The Day the Door Opened

Sandy Toms-Mann

The Day the Door Opened

Is dedicated to the incredible people who surround me, love me and support me every day. You are so, so loved.

<u>Chapter 1</u>

Hi, my name's Lacey. I'm eleven and I have this *huge* secret that I've never told anyone, not even my Mum. Well, I might tell my Mum, but I need to think about it first. And I'd certainly never tell my big sister Amy because she is so unbelievably annoying and doesn't deserve to know anything as awesome as what I'm going to share with you.

Actually, I have two secrets. Both are pretty fantastic and I'm not really sure which to tell you first. I suppose they're sort of tied together and if I start from the beginning… well, starting from the beginning is always a good idea, isn't it?

One Friday, last year, when I was in year five at Three Oaks Primary School, my Mum let me have my very first sleep over with my best friends Violet and Amelia. We've been besties since reception and we're totally going to still be best friends when we're, like, thirty-five and old and stuff.

Anyway, we were super excited, and we had it all planned out. Straight from school we were going back to my house to play outside by the pond (the tadpoles had just started growing legs and they were so funny to watch); then we were having Mum's mega-tasty sausage pie for tea before watching a movie with ice cream and popcorn in my bedroom. (I moved my room around to make it more spacious and set up beanbags and blankets as chairs). Then, after the film, we were allowed to talk for a bit before bedtime. Like I said, we were so excited. However, it didn't quite turn out as we had planned…

We made it through most of the plans (tadpole-watching, sausage-pie eating and ice cream enjoying) but whilst we were just tucking into sugary, crunchy popcorn, the weirdest, and I mean *weirdest,* thing happened.

"Lace, can we turn that light off?" Violet asked. "It's shining on the screen and I can't see properly."

"What light? I made sure all the lights were turned off when I pressed play," I replied, slightly confused.

"That one right at the-." She started to say back but stopped as she turned round to look. Her jaw dropped and her eyes grew so wide I could see the mysterious light reflected in them. I followed her gaze and felt my jaw drop as well. Without saying a word, without even turning around, I reached out to tap Amelia on the shoulder so that she'd look too.

As the three of us stared, I felt a chill run all the way up my spine and back down again.

My bed sits in the corner of my room. It's so tall that I have a desk under it for doing homework and drawing and stuff. It's really cute in there; I decked it out with fabulous multi-coloured fairy lights and put a sheet of shimmery, sparkly material down the end of the bed against the wall, opposite my desk. Normally it just sits there looking... well, looking like a piece of shimmery material but now, as we stared at it, a bright white light was glowing all the way around three edges of the fabric. There are no white lights under my bed so it shouldn't be glowing at all, let alone around the edges of the sheet but, even more strange, the sparkly fabric was now rippling gently as though a soft breeze was blowing through it.

Amelia's face lit up in a smile. "That looks amazing Lace, when did you put lights back there? It makes the shimmer really sparkle, I love it!"

"I… I've… n-n-not put any lights up there," I stammered back, feeling my hands go a little bit sweaty. (For about six nights in a row before this happened, I had dreamt that a white light was glowing up around my bed and I could hear voices in my room. It wasn't scary in my dreams but seeing it for real made me wonder whether I had actually been asleep, and that made me feel really nervous.)

"Stop mucking around you plonker, it looks brilliant. I wish I had a space like this in my room. Can I have a look at how you've done it?" Amelia's tinkling laugh danced across my room but it sounded distant; my ears felt thick as blood rushed through my head. I watched, frozen, as she crawled over the beanbags towards the strange light.

"Lacey, are you ok?" Violet asked, placing a soft, cool hand on my shoulder. It startled me so much I let out a little scream which, in turn, caused her to shriek as well. Us yelping had made Amelia jump too and she also found a squeak escaping her mouth. We all stared at each other, hands over our racing hearts, and as we all made eye contact, we started to laugh. I shook my head as I chuckled, shaking off the fear. Of course they had just been dreams; what else could it have been?

"Mum must have added them whilst I was at school today," I managed to say, as the laughter subsided. "I adore it, and the white lights won't clash with my multi-coloured ones. There must be a breeze coming in under my door. Stupid sister's probably got her window open again."

Violet and I clambered over the home-made cinema seats to where Amelia was; I wanted to have a closer look at how Mum had put the lights in as I was sure I'd used up all the plug sockets. 'I'm going to be really annoyed if she unplugged my computer.' I thought to myself.

We crawled towards the fluttering material, drawn to the light like bugs to a lamp.

Violet was the first to reach underneath my bed and, as the material lifted as though inflated by a gust of wind, she gasped and fell backwards. My eyes snapped to where she had been looking and my hand flew to my wide-open mouth.

As Violet was gasping and falling and I was covering

my mouth, Amelia whispered, "What the…?" as her face drained of colour, leaving her as white as a ghost.

Chapter 2

If you had looked behind the material that morning, you would have found a boring piece of plain white wall. But now? Well, now there was something quite different: a short beautiful, weathered door that was made of a rich dark brown wood. The door was held snugly in place by a smooth stone archway that was delicately decorated with spongy green moss. Set against the dark wood was a black, intricately designed handle with a grand-looking circular knocker.

As if *that* wasn't enough, there were broad blades of bright grass poking out from underneath, and we could clearly see where the white light and warm breeze were coming from.

"Umm, Lacey, why is there a door in your bedroom?" Violet gently asked so simply that she could have been asking what the time was. Looking back, I think it was the shock!

My mouth opened and closed like the orange goldfish

that lived downstairs, but no sound came out. In the end, I gave up trying and just shrugged.

I felt like I really should have been scared; a strange glowing doorway had appeared in my bedroom! But, oddly, I wasn't. It was mesmerising; I felt drawn to it; I couldn't look away.

Still crouched down from crawling over the beanbags, I moved slowly towards it as though in a trance. As I neared this peculiar spectacle, I felt Violet's cool hand tightly grip mine. However, even this unexpected contact was not enough to pull me out of my trance. As though from very far away, I heard Amelia murmur, "We're going through, aren't we?" Still not able to take my eyes off the strange new opening in my room, still holding Violet's hand, I nodded just once and reached my hand out to open the door.

The black, metal handle felt smooth and cool and it fitted neatly into my hand. I twisted it to the right; it turned easily and, with a heavy, satisfying 'thunk', the latch unhooked, and the door swung open towards me.

I screwed up my face against the bright light that filled the doorway. As I breathed in, my head was filled with the most delicious scent of warm honey blossom. I could hear the trickle of water somewhere beyond the blinding light and the delicate tweeting of birds.

It didn't take long for our eyes to get used to the light, and once they had adjusted, we could see that the green blades sticking out under the door were part of a much wider patch. Dotted all across the meadow, nestled in the luscious grass, were delicate white flowers with pale pink centres. The pretty flower heads danced gently in the breeze and brightly coloured butterflies flitted through the air, spinning and twisting together, creating a kaleidoscope of colour. Fat little bumblebees bees busily dipped in and out of the flowers and their faint hum could just be heard in the calm meadow.

I looked around to Amelia and Violet; our eyes locked onto each other's and, in that brief moment of contact, the unspoken message was clear – we were all ready to step out of the safety and normality of my bedroom and into this strange new world we had stumbled upon.

As one, we moved forwards onto the grass; it was soft, dry, and cool to touch. Once we were all through the short archway, we were able to stand up and look around properly.

The door we had come through was set into the biggest tree I had ever seen. Its bark ran vertically up and down the vast trunk and was ridged and rippled like an oak tree. I allowed my eyes to run up the tree trunk to the boughs above, and my breath was taken away by the greenness of the leaves. I'd never seen such a vivid, bright colour on a tree before! It was as though someone had put a 'vibrant' filter over our eyes and all the colours had become stronger, more fabulous.

"Are you frightened?" Violet asked in a tone so gentle we could have been in a library.

"I feel like I ought to be, but I don't feel scared at all. I feel quite peaceful," I replied, finally letting go of Violet's hand to run my palm across the rough texture of the tree.

"I was thinking the same thing!" Amelia breathed. Her eyes, as big as saucers, were roaming the clearing in which we found ourselves in as though she'd never seen anything like it. Which, I suddenly thought to myself, was exactly what she probably was thinking. That was certainly how I felt.

I drew my hand back down the enormous trunk and let it hang by my side. I could see a tree over the other side of the clearing that looked as though its bark was silvery and smooth; I wanted to touch it, to feel the softness. So many strands pouring down, covered in curved triangular leaves; it looked like nature's umbrella. As I got nearer the tree, I could see that the bark was indeed the most curious colour of silver; what I thought had been a trick of the light, turned out be real. And I was right in thinking the bark looked smooth; it was warm and wonderfully silky.

"Come and feel this tree guys, it's incredible!" I called to my friends. Neither replied though, so I turned to see where they were. Violet was crouched down on her hands and knees, nose almost flat to the floor.

"Vi, what on earth are you doing?!" I giggled.

She sat up, blushing slightly. "Come and smell these white flowers. Seriously, it's, like, the nicest smell I've ever smelt." I've always enjoyed the scent of different flowers (roses are my absolute favourite), so I left the silky-smooth tree and went to join Violet on the floor. As I bent down over the ground, my long blonde hair fell over my face like a sheet and it tickled my nose. Once I had tucked my locks behind my ears I was able to tell that she was right: they were breath-taking. Clearly, these flowers were responsible for the smell we'd experienced when we'd opened the door.

"Amelia, come and look at-." Violet started to say but she stopped mid-sentence. I looked up to see why. We both scanned the clearing but there was no sign of Amelia.

"Amelia?" I called, quickly standing up, a shot of panic shooting across my chest. "*Amelia*?"

Violet joined in too, calling "Amelia?"

"Yeh?" came her voice from behind us. We both span round so fast we nearly collided and I grabbed Violet's shoulder to stop myself falling over.

"Where were you?" I asked with a sigh of relief. I realised that, since stepping though the door, I'd been too wrapped up in my own wonder to know what my friends were doing.

"Don't panic; I was only round the other side of the tree. We do have a slight problem though," she responded.

"What?" Violet and I said at the same time.

"Well... it's just... well... the door's disappeared. We

can't get back to your bedroom, Lace."

<u>Chapter 3</u>

It took a moment for Amelia's words to register in my thoughts but, as soon as they had, I ran across the springy grass towards her and frantically searched around the base of the broad tree.

I heard the rustling of Violet's rapid footsteps approaching as she, too, joined in the hunt for what we knew to be our only way back home.

The three of us were practically running around the tree constantly brushing our hands up and down the trunk trying to find the handle, the edge of the door, anything.

Violet was the first to slump to the ground, back against the tree, knees drawn up to her chest. Amelia had barely spotted her, stopping just before she went crashing over and I ran straight into Amelia's back.

"Ouch!" I said thickly, rubbing my nose.

"Sorry," Amelia replied, "I nearly tripped over Violet."

Like a short row of toppling dominoes, Amelia sat down next to Violet and I followed. We must have been a sorry sight: arms around legs, leaning up against a gigantic tree, pale with shock and fear.

"What are we going to do?" Whispered Violet, with a tremor in her voice. "My Mum… she'll be so worried. What if we never make it home? I'm all she has and now we have basically disappeared and this'll break her heart and what about school and what are we going to eat and what if there are bears or scary things that will eat us. What if-" She was clearly spiraling into panic, so I shuffled round to be in between my friends, draped my arm around her shoulders and pulled her towards me in a warm hug. However, I had no words of comfort to offer as these thoughts were tumbling through my head too. (Except the one about Mum; she's got Amy and Dad. And maybe the bears... not sure why Violet was worried about bears.)

Amelia, on the other hand, has always had this wonderful ability to see the good in everyone, the positive in everything and the light in every dark. "Take a breath Vi, this could be the best adventure of our lives! We're here together, this place is more beautiful than anything we've ever seen and we've not even moved more than ten metres from where we came in! Not to mention the fact that you have no idea whether we're actually stuck here. Ooo, also!" She got excited now, "Maybe time has stopped back home! How cool would that be?! We'll be lost here but then we'll get back home, and it'll be like we were never away! See, you'll be fine." She finished with such a triumphant look anyone would think she'd just solved world hunger. Violet, on the other hand, looked far from convinced.

"I'm not sure I wholly agree with what Amelia's just said," I uttered," but I am certainly glad we came through the door together and I wasn't on my own. Just think if you guys hadn't been at my house tonight and I came through by myself! That would have been awful. If I had to get lost with anyone in a strange, unknown place, I'd choose you two every time." Violet leaned her head down onto my shoulder and Amelia followed suit on my other side. We sat there, silently, for some time just looking around at the beauty that surrounded us, drinking in the colours and textures. I watched multi-coloured butterflies (far brighter than I'd seen before) flit merrily around, dancing to the tunes only they could hear. Violet's panicked breathing was finally subsiding and I could feel her body relaxing as the tension eased. I could feel the fear starting to subside inside me, too. 'Maybe this is all just a crazy dream. Maybe we will be ok like Amelia said, after all she is usually right.' I thought to myself. But just as I was thinking these calming thoughts, Amelia's whole body tensed, and her head shot up like a meerkat.

"What's that-" I began to ask.

"Shh!" She interrupted in a harsh whisper. "I can hear something coming."

Our heads snapped up too, ears straining. We heard it coming, rustling through the bushes over to our right. Scoring a ten out of ten for perfect synchronisation, we turned our heads towards the greenery, breath held in apprehension and fear.

Chapter 4

The bush trembled harder and harder and we could hear a strange sort of grunting sound coming from within, as though someone was struggling to pass through the thick tangle of branches. We waited and waited, watching, each of us secretly hoping it wasn't the bear Violet had been scared of. Hoping that it would be a friendly someone. Hoping that they might be able to help us get home.

However, what came out of the bush surprised us all.

The first obvious thing was that it was not a person; it was some sort of animal, and the second thing was that it was certainly not an animal any of us had ever seen before.   .

Coming out of the hedge was… a tail. A short, stumpy sort of tail that was white all the way along until the tuft of hair at the end which was, if you can believe it, rainbow-striped and fluffy. In my shock I found myself imagining that if the tail had not been pushed backwards through a bush, it would probably be sleek and rather soft to touch.

Attached to this extraordinary tail was a white wiggly bottom, then a pair of blue-hoofed legs, closely followed by a stout, round little belly. Pushing itself through the branches were a second pair of blue-hoofed legs and then, finally, a head which made all of us gasp loudly. The creature turned round and, as it spotted us, froze to the spot like a deer caught in headlights. There, stood in front of us, as real as any of the trees surrounding it, was…

"A unicorn!" I breathed, utterly spellbound.

Amelia gave a small, snorting laugh. To be fair, I could see why. The little creature must have stood no more than waist-tall and having come through a hedge backwards, it's white fur stood up on end poking out in all different directions; a rainbow mane was decidedly ruffled and beautiful sea-blue eyes stared at us with a look of embarrassment at being found backing out of a hedge.

There was a moment of absolute stillness where we were all frozen to the spot, us staring at the unicorn and the unicorn staring at us.

The unicorn finally broke the silence. "Err, hi." None of us replied, we just continued staring. The silence dragged on, and the unicorn gave itself a shake as though trying to flatten down its unruly fur. Then, clearly bored of our staring match, the colourful creature plopped its rainbow-tipped bottom onto the floor and used a front hoof to scratch its chest. This scene must have played out for a good few minutes before I finally gave myself a mental shake and spoke: "Hi. I'm Lacey. These are my friends, Violet and Amelia. We've never met a unicorn before. To be honest we've never been *here* before. We're not even sure where *here* is. We came through a door in this tree but then it disappeared and we are not at all sure what to do about getting home. We've never met a unicorn before. I've said that already haven't I? I'm just really surprised. And you talk. When I was little I always wished unicorns were real but I'd always thought of them as being big and tall like a horse and I never thought they'd talk." I stopped and took a much-needed breath. I could feel my cheeks tinge red as the unicorn looked at me with wide eyes from surprise at the sudden change from absolute silence to a hail storm of words pouring out of my mouth.

"Alright there Lacc?!" Amelia murmured in my ear.

"Sorry," I apologised. "I'm not sure where all that came from. I think I'm just really surprised. I've never met a unicorn before."

"So you keep saying," replied the unicorn with a smirk. "My name's Pedro. I knew you'd be coming but you're earlier than expected, hence why you had to witness my unfortunate entrance into the waiting area." Pedro gave himself another little shake, like a wet dog. "This is so embarrassing, but could you please come and pat my fur down? It is so uncomfortable when it's all sticking up like this. Usually I'm able to roll it flat on the grass in private but…"

"Err yeh, ok." I agreed, as I stood up to make my way over to the little creature. His glistening white fur was as soft as the richest velvet and spread the most soothing warmth throughout my body; I felt it flow through my finger-tips, flooding my veins from the top of my head right down to the tips of my toes. I worked the fur flat all along his little warm body right the way down until I reached the tip of his beautifully bright rainbow tail. When I'd finished, I looked at my hand and was pleasantly surprised to see a glittering rainbow disappearing. I caught Pedro looking at me and, as our eyes met, there was a strange connection, a bond, an understanding forming. He gave the smallest of nods at me and I gave a small smile of recognition back.

The calming moment was suddenly splintered by Amelia's voice: "Hang on," she barked. "You said you knew we'd be coming. How did you know?"

With a jolt, I realised she was correct and turned my gaze immediately back to Pedro to await his answer.

"The Queen called for you," Pedro responded simply, as if that cleared everything up for us. We went back to staring at him.

Pedro sighed and scratched his forehead with a small hoof. "Yes, alright. I suppose that made absolutely no sense at all to you did it. Follow me." He gave us a little smile, turned on his hooves, and trotted off around the clearing and disappeared between two thick, emerald-green bushes.

I looked down at my two friends, who were still sitting at the base of the tree through which we had arrived. I held out both my hands, one to each of them, which they grasped and pulled themselves up to standing.

Violet's dark hazel eyes were filled with concern and her slender, pale fingers worried a hunk of her long purpley-black hair. In contrast, Amelia's bluebell-blue eyes shone brightly with excitement out of her olive skin, and her aubern pixie-cut stood on end where she'd run her hands through it too often.

"Shall we?" I asked, a slight smile breaking across my face. "We're here now aren't we? The door's gone so why not have what could be the best adventure of our lives?"

A small smile brightened Violet's worried face and a huge grin spread across Amelia's.

"Let's go girls," Amelia announced, and the three of us stepped as one across the honey blossom scented clearing after Pedro the rainbow unicorn.

Chapter 5

As we passed through the tickly hedge, we found ourselves in a large, dim cave; the sound of trickling water (that we'd heard through the door) became louder and we could see a waterfall cascading over another opening in the rock.

Pedro was standing in the centre of the gloom patiently waiting for us to catch up. I gazed around the echoey space giving my eyes time to get used to the darkness. A thrill of pleasure ran through me: the ceiling was speckled with hundreds, maybe thousands of silver pinpricks as though it was a full night sky. It was so beautiful; I felt like I could stare at it forever.

Pedro gestured to a row of large, squashy cushions set along one side of the cave wall and said, "Sit down girls. Would you like a drink?"

"Err yeh sure, thanks." I responded, whilst Amelia jumped in with, "Absolutely! Yes please."

Without a sound, a tiny figure scurried out of the darkness in front of us, shot over to the waterfall, filled three clear glasses with tumbling water and carefully brought them over to us. As I reached out a slightly trembling hand to accept the drink, I was able to get a really good look at what was serving us. The best way to describe it would be to say that it was a cross between a cotton-wool ball and a fluffy dandelion (the ones you blow into the wind): bright, royal blue with three green stalks coming out of it (one from the top its head and two where you would expect arms to be). At the end of each of these stalks was a smaller fluffy ball but this time, the one above its head was a dazzling purple and the ones at its arms were a candyfloss pink. From the fluffy balls where its arms would be, sprouted little hands that were grasping the tray of drinks. It had black sparkly eyes, no nose and the cutest little smile that made you feel that this creature, whatever it was, could only be friendly.

Once we had taken our drinks, the fluffy ball thing spun round and disappeared back into the darkness. As it hurried off, I could just see, poking out of the bottom of its main fluffy ball, two little rapidly moving feet, slapping gently against the damp rock floor.

After we had all drank the water we wanted, Pedro parked himself on another cushion opposite us and began to explain why we were there. I sat, rapt, unable to look away as he spoke with a soothing, melodious voice.

"You find yourselves in a place called Mostomsia. It is a kingdom that exists in a reality parallel to yours. For as long as anyone can remember, it has been ruled over by either a king or a queen. We value our water-folk as much as our land dwellers, so we alternate between a leader from the water and from the land. Currently, we are ruled by Queen Beatrice from the water, who took over the ruling from Queen Alexia of the land. When Queen Beatrice dies, the crown will be passed to the heir of the land throne, Prince Thomas. When he dies, the crown will go back to the sea and so on and so forth. With me so far?"

We all nodded mutely so Pedro continued.

"Our people have lived peacefully for many, many years but sadly we now find ourselves in conflict."

"Why? What's happened?" Amelia interrupted, eager to understand our reason for being there.

"Well," Pedro carried on. "No-one knows how long

our rulers will live for; our life spans are very different from those in your reality. It turns out that Prince Thomas has grown weary of waiting and has taken matters into his own hands. He has kidnapped the Queen's daughter, Princess Isla, to force the Queen to abdicate the thrown and have the power handed over to him."

"That's dreadful! What a horrible thing to do!" Violet cried out. "But what does that have to do with us?"

"The Queen is, naturally, distraught at the loss of her daughter and is working tirelessly to help bring Isla back home safely. Alas, nothing has worked and so she has been forced to seek assistance from elsewhere… you. Magic is limited in our world; we try to use it only in matters of emergency. Queen Beatrice cast the Succurro Spell out into the realities surrounding ours in the hope that help would come. It was cast some weeks ago now and we were beginning to lose hope. See, the spell doesn't land straight away; it moves around searching for the right place, the right people."

"So, it's no coincidence that the door opened up in my bedroom this evening? The spell thinks that we are the right people for... hold on! I've seen light in my bedroom all last week and heard voices! Has it been waiting until my friends were with me before opening properly?" I asked with excitement, the penny dropping.

"Yes, that is exactly right." Pedro nodded to me. "I was sent to fetch you each evening, which is why you heard voices and saw the light, but the door never properly appeared until today because it wasn't quite ready. Now, it deemed you three worthy and opened to let you through."

There was a pause as the three of us let Pedro's story sink into our already saturated minds.

"So your Suc-something Spell has whizzed around the universe looking for someone to help your Queen get her daughter back, ended up in Lacey's bedroom because it thinks *we* are the right people for the job?!" Amelia sounded incredulous.

I sat back against the cool, damp wall of the cave and let out a long, breath of awe and confusion. How could three girls from primary school possibly be chosen to save an alternate reality from a power-hungry prince?! What on earth had we walked into?

"No one can possibly fathom the workings of magic but, yes, that is exactly what is going on here. You three have been chosen by the Succurro Spell to come here and help save our world from being ruled by a greedy monster. Like I said, we had started to give up so now there is no time to lose. We must make haste to the palace of Queen Beatrice and start you on your journey." With that, Pedro stood up on his four sparkly hooves and looked at us expectantly.

"Well I don't suppose we can really let them down, can we?" I murmured to my friends. Violet looked back at me, apprehension and fear etched on her pretty face but, despite that, there was a hint of bravery as she jutted her chin out and gave one, firm nod of acceptance. Amelia, obviously, had already jumped up and was bobbing on the balls of her feet, ready to race off after the unicorn who had, we suddenly realised, disappeared through the glistening waterfall. I put my hands on my knees and pushed my body up to standing; I reached out to take Violet's hand and, together, we turned and marched after Pedro, once again stepping through into the unknown.

Chapter 6

Amelia was the first to pass through the tumbling water. I was about to follow her but stopped: I knew how nervous and frightened Violet would be feeling and didn't want her to be left alone in the cave. I stepped to the side and gave my quiet, gentle friend a smile of encouragement and a squeeze of her hand before she, too, left the cave.

I took one last glance at the star-speckled ceiling before turning to face the sheet of falling water. I mentally braced myself for the coldness of the water, took a deep breath, clenched my fists in preparation and walked into the waterfall.

It was like stepping into a luxury shower in the most expensive hotel you can think of. The water was falling fast, yet when it hit my skin it felt no harsher than if someone was throwing cotton wool at me. Where I had expected to feel icy shards pummelling me, I was surprised to feel such a pleasantly comfortable warmth that I didn't want to walk out the other side. I briefly wondered whether my friends had

had the same experience.

Once I left the delights of the waterfall and walked out after Violet and Amelia, two things happened. One: I realised that, even though I had felt the water penetrate my clothes, plaster my hair to my head, I was already completely dry. Two: I could tell from the looks on my friends' faces, as they both stared back at the waterfall, that they had indeed felt the same as me.

I looked around where I had come out and saw we were in a clearing almost identical to the one we had been in on the other side of the cave. It was just as vibrant and colourful and, I realised, had no obvious exit for us to take. So how were we going to leave?

"Visitors through the waterfall always have that reaction, but I must insist that we get a move on; there really isn't a moment to lose." Pedro beckoned us with one of his shiny hooves, turned around and headed off towards a towering mass of ferns surrounded by bushes and trees.

"How are we supposed to get out? I don't see a door and I don't fancy going backwards through a hedge like he did!" Amelia whispered to me. I looked at her and shrugged in response.

However, just before Pedro would have been covered in leaves, he stopped. Like obedient puppies, we stopped behind him waiting quietly, apprehensive to see what would happen next. Pedro crouched down and gave his whole body a little shake before rearing up on his hind legs and facing the patch of ferns. Once he was steady, he began waving his front hooves as though conducting an orchestra through a piece of frantic music. (I imagined the Flight of the Bumble-Bee!) I could feel a bubble of laughter building in my tummy as I watched the fluffy rainbow of his tail wiggling around as he jiggled. Next to me, I felt Violet give a little quiver of laughter and heard Amelia trying to hold in a desperate-to-escape giggle. As quickly as my bubble of laughter had grown, it was popped and replaced by a fizzing of awe and excitement.

The little unicorn had set his front hooves back on the ground and was watching as something as beautiful as it was amazing unfurl in front of him. Not for the first time that day, my jaw dropped in wonder.

The hedge was trembling; I could hear the hush, hush, hush of the leaves as they whispered their secrets to us. The ferns were growing, reaching for the sky. Their tiny, snail-like fists of leaves were opening and stretching as though waking from a deep, peaceful slumber, and out of each fist came a small glowing ball of light, no bigger than a pea. The balls of light floated, shivering slightly, above the ferns as they continued to open, growing, and growing. I couldn't believe what I was seeing. The whole thing can only have lasted for two or three glorious minutes and when it was over, the ferns had created a stunning, glowing, luscious-green entrance to a pathway.

The unicorn moved off through the new gateway and had gone a few metres before realising that the three of us were rooted to the spot, jaws still hanging loose, eyes like saucers.

"Come on, come on," he gently chivvied, smiling at the looks on our faces.

Naturally, Amelia was the first to follow Pedro and, again, I encouraged Violet to go ahead of me. Through the fern-archway, the path looked dark and slightly daunting and I saw Violet nervously twisting her hair through her fingers again. She paused at the top of the path and I could see her shoulders raise in a deep breath.

"Hi, My name's Titch. Are you a bit scared?" came the tiniest, highly-pitched voice I'd ever heard.

Violet's head whipped round in surprise and I flicked my head back and forth searching for the source of the voice.

"I'm here!" came the voice again. "Look, just above your right ear."

We both looked at her ear and Violet let out a little squeal of surprise. There, dangling above her, was a little black spider hanging from a delicate, silvery thread. There were several bright white eyes shining out of its fuzzy black body and, bizarrely, the corners of its eyes were all turned up as though it was smiling. I secretly felt very glad we'd already heard a unicorn talk; a talking spider as our first magical encounter may have been a bit too much!

"Oh!" exclaimed Violet, hand fluttering over her pounding heart. "Hello. You startled me but yes, I am a bit nervous actually. I'm not a huge fan of the dark if

I'm honest." There was a pause as the spider and Violet eyed each other but suddenly the spider scurried back up the thread and disappeared.

"Oh. I wonder where he went." Violet sounded slightly disappointed. "Did you see the tiny rainbow flow between us? That was weird. It felt like we had some sort of connection. That probably sounds crazy."

"No!" I blurted back. "I'm so glad you said that! I had the same thing with Pedro when we met back in the clearing and he asked me to smooth down his fur. It was weird!"

"Really?! Wow! At least he stuck around though. I wonder why Titch disappeared like that. I didn't say anything offensive, did I?"

"No you didn't. I don't know. Sorry." I replied, with sympathy in my voice.

We didn't have to wonder for long though.

"I'm back! And I've brought something to help you." came Titch's voice. We looked behind us and Titch was swinging through the plants like Spiderman, with the many, many tiny orbs of light from the ferns floating behind him. The little spider jumped down onto Violet's shoulder and the lights flowed around us, down into the tunnel and then paused as though waiting for us to follow. As soon as we started to walk down the leafy tunnel, now gently lit by the orbs, they moved on ahead of us, lighting the way. In no time at all, we had caught up with Amelia and Pedro.

The leafy green tunnel zigzagged its way down what seemed to be the side of a mountain. The glowing orbs bobbed around us, lighting the way and I could hear the intermittent chatter of Violet and Titch in front of me.

After what felt like an hour of walking, the ground levelled out and there, ahead of us, was the end of the tunnel.

<u>Chapter 7</u>

I could see the bright blue sky, lit by a brilliant sun ahead and, there, shimmering below, was the sea, sparkling and dancing.

The tunnel led out onto a dusty-yellow dry, sandy beach. We took our shoes off to feel the sand between our toes as Pedro led us towards the turquoise waters; the sand felt pleasantly warm on the soles of our feet.

Waiting at the edge of the water, bobbing about in the shallows, was one enormous, dusky-pink clam shell. As we approached, it opened to reveal a large interior with squashy, dark-red cushions at the bottom.

"This shell will take us down to the palace where Queen Beatrice will be waiting." We clambered into the shell, that smelled faintly of fish, and it closed around us. A large handful of the orbs from the ferns had followed each of us into the shells and the cushions were plush and squishy, making the journey comfortable and warm.

Whilst we travelled down through the sea the shell rocked gently, and we talked about not a whole lot really, each of us wrapped up in our own thoughts.

The lull of the travelling shell was soothing; the dim lighting and comfortable cushions meant it wasn't long before my eye lids felt heavy and I felt myself drifting off into an easy sleep.

I've no idea how long I was out for, but the next thing I knew, Pedro was using his colourful mane to tickle me awake (he did say he was very careful not to poke me in the eye with the unicorn horn!).

"We're here." he told me as I awoke, blinking slowly.

The shell opened and Amelia, Violet, Pedro and I stood up, stretched and looked around at where the shell had dropped us.

We had landed on a pale pink and white marble floor that was pleasantly cool against our feet. From the edges of the wide, oval floor, stretching high over our heads was a clear, dome through which we could see all the marvels and wonders of the deep sea. Hundreds of colourful fish zipped around in twinkling shoals; playful seahorses galloped around in their herds and a shimmering fever of sting rays soared over head.

A door we had not noticed opened with a clang at one end of the egg-shaped room spewing out of it a group of six mermaids… well mermen guards, actually.

Amelia squealed in delight (she has always loved mermaids although never thought them to be actually real!). The mermen had scaly blue tails, bare chests and each carried a trident. If they hadn't been smiling, they would have been rather intimidating. Thankfully the smile was warm and friendly, crinkling the corners of their vivid-purple eyes.

"Let us extend to you a warm welcome, friends. We have waited so long for your arrival. Come, follow, our great Queen is waiting eagerly to meet you." The leading merman beckoned to us with an elegant hand. Our feet slapped gently on the floor as we walked across the great hall and we followed the merguards through a maze of passageways.

"How come there's no water here in the palace? How do you all move around?" I asked, interested in how the mermaids were able to apparently float through the air.

"It's magic." One of the merguards called back.

"I suppose I could have guessed that really!" I chuckled.

We carried on walking until we came to a vast green door, sparkling with emeralds and sapphires. I glanced over my shoulder to where we had come from and was pleasantly surprised to see the orbs from the ferns were still following us! It was oddly comforting and made me feel safe.

One of our guards rapped on the door three times; we could hear the knocks echoing throughout the room beyond. When the echoes had died down, we heard a loud, clear voice call "Enter!" and the door opened inwards with a gentle whoosh.

Chapter 8

The guards stood back to let us enter the room and I heard Titch murmur to Violet, "It's ok. I've heard the Queen is really kind and I'm right here with you."

The door opened into a long, wide, light room with a black and white chess board floor. Along the floor, every few paces, were grand statues of mer-people wearing various designs of crowns, and along the walls were glorious paintings depicting scenes of joy and happiness. Above our heads, arching in a great half-pipe shape was another window running the length of the hall that allowed us to, once again, see out into the ocean beyond. At the end of hall, gazing up through the ocean's depths was the most extraordinary person I have ever seen. To begin with, she was a mermaid so already I was in awe. Her tail was a periwinkle blue with lilac-purple fins fluttering gently at the end. She wore a scalloped skirt of duck egg blue and a pretty pink top with orange and lemon-yellow ruffles over her delicate, thin shoulders.

Well that all sounds quite normal, I hear you say. Let me tell you that if this was topped with, say, a blonde or brown head of hair then yes I would have agreed with you. However, flowing like a waterfall from the top of her head down to mid-tail was thick, shiny hair of midnight black and hot pink in broad stripes.

She turned to face us as she heard our footsteps echoing around the room (I was suddenly very aware that we'd all left our shoes in the shell). Worry, grief and pain were etched into her beautiful, china-doll face. Queen Beatrice was quite the most gorgeous person I'd ever had the fortune to meet.

Taking Pedro's lead, we all sank into deep bows to honour her majesty. As we stood, a weak smile crept across her face, but it didn't quite touch the sadness in her eyes. She floated towards us and reached out her arms to embrace us warmly.

"Children, you are finally here. Thank you for having the courage and bravery to help me, my kingdom, my family…" she paused and wiped away a tear that trickled a lonely path down her perfect face,"… my daughter."

"Your highness." Pedro began. "We are all here ready to serve you and your kingdom. The children have followed me freely and willingly, having taken their first steps of bravery coming through the doorway into our world. I have already formed a Bond with one child, and Titch, a spider, has formed a Bond with another. We will both loyally join the children on their journey. My hope is that the third child will form her Bond soon after we return to the surface."

"My darling Pedro," the Queen laid a hand softly on his head. "Word of your strength, courage and love has reached me even down here under the waters. Please present your child so I may thank her."

Pedro turned to me with a smile on his kindly face. I stepped forward and sank into a second bow to pay my respect to the beautiful Queen before me.

"I am Lacey, Your Majesty." I offered her a smile, which she gracefully returned.

"Lacey. Welcome, and thank you. I feel you are loyal and kind. These are good qualities in a person. It is a pleasure to meet you." I gave a small smile and nod, then stepped back into line alongside my friends.

"Titch, please bring your child to me."

Violet stepped forwards with Titch balancing on her shoulder, where he'd been since returning with the orbs.

"Your Highness," Titch squeaked. "I present to you, Violet." Violet also sank into a bow before smiling shyly at the Queen. Titch attempted a many-legged bow on her shoulder, which made me smile.

"Violet, Titch. It is a pleasure and an honour to meet you. Thank you for offering your services to our troubled lands. I see within you fear and worry but I also see great strength and bravery. Again, thank you." The Queen bobbed a nod to Violet who then stepped back next to me.

"And finally we have you, my dear." Queen Beatrice smiled at Amelia. "Come, child." She beckoned with her pale fingers and Amelia stepped forwards, the last of us to bow to the Queen.

"Amelia, your Majesty," my friend spoke gently.

"Ah, Amelia. I sense positivity and joy is strong within you. This will help you keep your friends on the path of this journey. Your Bond will find you soon after you are back on dry land, of this I am sure. Thank you for coming to help." Smiles and nods were exchanged, and then Amelia came to stand beside me and Violet.

"And so, to business. You will return to the shores by

shell. My daughter, Isla, was last seen near the enclosed cove on the north shore of the island. Sadly, that is all the information I can offer. Beware though, Prince Thomas is clever and sneaky; in the letter he sent to me explaining what he had done and why, he informed me that no-one will be able to find him as he has laid a series of traps and tricks designed to capture or hurt, or both. My children, this will be a perilous journey and you must take every care to keep yourselves safe so you can return home to your families."

Violet and I looked at each other, mirrored expressions of anxiousness and fear imprinted on our faces.

"When you have found my daughter and rescued her from the wicked Prince, use this shell to call me, and I will send transport to bring you back. Use this wisely though as its powers of communication are limited; you must only use it when you are absolutely sure you are ready to return." The beautiful Queen reached both her slender hands behind her head and unclasped the delicate necklace that hung around her graceful neck. She put the shell to her lips and closed her eyes in a brief moment of quiet, and then held it out in her open palm. We watched in amazed interest as the tiny pink, glittery shell floated off her hand and hung, suspended in the air. We all watched, waiting and then the shell quivered, spun slowly around three times and flew towards me. I held up my opened hand to pluck the shell out of the air.

"Lacey, the shell has chosen you. Wear it with pride, guard it safely and use it wisely." The Queen graced me with a small smile that did reach her eyes this time. "And now, you must go. Farewell, my brave children and I look forward to your safe return with Isla."

The mer-guards circled around our small group and guided us back through the passageways to where we had first stepped out into the palace.

Before we clambered back into the shell, the lead mer-guard shook each of our hands in turn, wished us good luck and then, finally, saluted us all as the top half of the shell closed us in.

Chapter 9

There was a thick, heavy silence as our transport moved off. The tension oozing from each of us was so thick you could have touched it. After a few minutes of total quiet, Violet broke it by murmuring, "I want to go home," in such a small, wobbly voice that it made my heart ache for her. I saw Titch reach down a long slender (and hairy) leg to wipe a solitary tear off Violet's cheek.

"I know it sounded scary Vi, but I'm sure no-one would ever send kids off to do a job that was so dangerous they couldn't do it. The Queen's spell chose us! It must think we can succeed, or it wouldn't have opened the door to us. I really do think we'll be ok," Amelia piped up, positive as always. I personally wasn't sure I agreed but I wasn't going to say anything as I didn't want to upset Violet anymore. Vi's face echoed my thoughts though: she didn't look at all convinced.

I can't have been hiding my feelings as well as I thought I was though, because Pedro laid his beautiful head in my lap and looked up at me with his kind eyes. I stroked his fur and at once I felt both comforted and inspired.

"Violet, I think Amelia's right, you know," I spoke out, with new-found confidence. "If the spell didn't think we could do it, it wouldn't have chosen us. It's as though we are meant to succeed. We just have to focus, help and support each other, and we'll be fine!" I finished with a big smile that was gladly returned by Amelia; Violet was able to offer up a small smile, but she still didn't seem one hundred percent on board.

"Yeh. I guess," she said with a shrug.

The shell's passengers returned to silent contemplation. This time, my mind was too busy to allow me to drop off to sleep so I continued to gain strength and courage from stroking Pedro, and I could see Titch and Violet having a muted conversation. Amelia just sat on her cushion with her eyes closed but I could tell she wasn't actually asleep.

After some time, we came to an abrupt stop and I could hear the waves knocking gently against the shell. The top half lifted once more, and I could see that we were back on land but on a different beach from the one we had left earlier. The sand on this beach was like black glitter, sparkling under the bright sun. The shape of the beach was a semi-circle surrounded by vast, luscious trees and plants. It was a little cove.

"There must be a volcano around here somewhere. They produce black sand. My brother was telling us about it when he was learning about volcanoes at school. It's eerie but ever so beautiful." Amelia announced.

"You're absolutely right Amelia," Pedro replied. "There is a volcano right up ahead. It hasn't erupted for hundreds of years now; I think it's been classified as extinct."

We all stood on the beach looking around.

"What on earth do we do now?" asked Violet.

There was silence as we contemplated the answer to this. Having never saved more than a snail on the pavement before, we weren't really sure how you went about saving a whole world.

"Umm. Well. How about we err… fan out and look for clues? Queen Beatrice said that Isla was last seen here so maybe there will be something that will help us?" I offered. Each of my companions nodded at me and wandered off to search the black-sanded cove for clues of the missing Princess.

Pedro and I set off together, moving slowly and carefully, walking a grid across the black beach. As we reached the tree line, we could hear Amelia puffing and panting; we looked over to see what she was doing.

"Amelia, what on earth are you doing?!" I exclaimed, as I watched her rooting around on her hands and knees with her head buried in a lime-green bush. Due to the head-in-a-hedge thing, I wasn't able to understand her muffled response. Thankfully, all became clear moments later as she gave an almighty tug, flew backwards and landed on her back with a pink cushion clutched tightly to her tummy.

It turned out it wasn't actually a cushion at all, which was made clear when the pink 'thing' gave a squeal and a grunt and rolled onto the sand next to my sweaty friend. Pedro and I just stood staring, gobsmacked at the sight in front of us.

The pink 'thing-not-a-cushion' was in fact a little pink pig with a sparkly pink belly. I gasped and jumped back as the pig sprouted a pair of beautiful white wings and took itself up into the air before landing on its little trotters in front of Amelia.

"Are you ok? I hope you didn't hurt yourself, but thank you loads for getting me out of that hole. I was very stuck!" Amelia stared open-mouthed as the pig spoke to her, holding out its front trotter to help pull her up. Brushing herself free of sand now that she was upright, Amelia pushed a hand through her hair before taking a deep breath.

"You can fly. Pigs really can fly." She said dumbly, still staring.

"I know, pretty cool right?" The pig replied. "I'm the only one that can as far as I know. None of my brothers or sisters can. I think maybe my great-great-great something or other Grandad could but other than that, it's just me. I'm Piggins by the way." Piggins held out his trotter to shake hands with Amelia and offered her a smile that spread right up past his twinkly eyes to his floppy pink ears.

Amelia held out her hand in return and I was thrilled to see the pale rainbow flow between my friend and Piggins. There was a pause as the two held eye contact, the bond being formed between them.

"I'm Amelia. Pleased to meet you. Are you my Bond now? Queen Beatrice said she thought I'd meet my Bond soon after we got back to land."

"I am. And very happy to be." replied Piggins. "How do you know who Queen Beatrice is? I know you're not even from this land!"

Before Amelia could answer, however, Violet's shrill cry of "I've found something!" echoed across the small beach. We all turned to see her and, once we'd spotted her, we all raced across the sand to find out what she had discovered.

"Look!" she gasped, as we reached her. Her face was glowing with excitement and pride as she pointed a long finger at something on the sand. We looked at what she was pointing to and joined her in her excitement.

There, half buried in the sand, was a piece of grey rock covered in dark green, crispy seaweed. Dried onto the rock, glistening in the light, were shining fish scales. I bent over to get a closer look and found something slightly buried in the sand next to the rock. I picked it up and held open my palm to show the others. Nestled in my hand was a silver bracelet with a tiny charm in the shape of a crown. I lifted the bracelet closer to my face so I could inspect the charm and there, etched into the crown, was the letter 'I'.

"This must be Princess Isla's!" I squealed. "Look, there's an I on the crown. And these scales on the rock must have come from her tail. That horrible man must have dragged her across this rock. Maybe she left the bracelet here so someone could find her!"

"We need to see if we can find any more scales or clues and work out which direction she was taken in." piped up Titch's tiny voice.

"Good idea." declared Amelia. So, again we all set off along the tree line, carefully inspecting every inch of ground and tree, desperately hoping to find something that would bring us closer to Princess Isla.

The warm sun beat down on the back of my neck whilst Pedro and I worked our way along the black sand. His rainbow fur looked so beautiful in the bright light and I took great comfort in running my hand through its softness. At one point, I stood up to stretch my slightly aching back and I glanced towards the sun to see the reflected light dancing on the gently rolling waves. As usual, the sun made my nose tickle and I turned back towards the greenery as I sneezed loudly. Pedro jumped about a foot off the floor but as I lifted my head, something caught my eye. Just over to my left was a shimmer that was quite out of place on the green leaves. I rushed over and was delighted to see another small collection of dried scales glistening in the sun.

"Over here!" I bellowed across the cove to the others, who rushed towards me like a herd of cows.

"There!" I pointed to what I had found and excitement rippled through our small group.

"There's another bit!" cried Amelia rushing to another bush over to the left.

"Look at this! I've found a path." oinked Piggins. For a moment, none of us could see where he was but then he appeared from behind the bush I'd found. "This is like a secret entrance hidden between these two plants. She must have been taken up there."

We all scuttled behind the bush to see what Piggins was talking about and, sure enough, we found ourselves at the beginning of a stony path that led off through the forest beyond, winding and twisting like a giant snake.

Amelia turned to start off up the track, but Violet grabbed Amelia's arm and pulled her back.

"Wait! Queen Beatrice said there would be tricks and traps and stuff. What if there is one here on the beginning of the path to stop us going up it?" Violet's eyebrows knotted together with concern.

"Why don't we all throw sticks at it and see if they trigger anything?" suggested Titch in his teeny-weeny voice. There was a pause as we all considered this and, with no other better ideas, we all grabbed a stick and prepared to launch.

"Ready?" Asked Titch. We nodded in response. "One... two... three!"

We hurled our sticks and waited with bated breath. Nothing happened.

"Right. Ok. There we go. Let's crack on." With that, Amelia promptly walked off up the path. Piggins jogged after her and Violet and I hurried after them with Pedro's hooves crunching on the stones.

Chapter 10

As we marched up the path, the canopy, created by the forest either side, loomed over us like a vast, green monster. The further we got from the beach and the more the monster enveloped us, the darker and colder it got, until our skin was all goose bumps. Our bodies shivered. Every few minutes one of us would gratefully recognise a small patch of dried mermaid scales, boosting our resolve to keep going through the intimidating gloom.

"C-c-c-can we s-s-s-stop a minute," Violet requested after a while, through chattering teeth, "I just n-n-n-need a quick break."

We all stopped, and Violet sank down to perch on the top of a mangled tree stump. The rest of us gathered closely, trying to keep warm.

Suddenly, there was a rustle in the foliage behind where Violet was sitting. We all froze; hearts pounding, eyes wide. I found my hand slowly reaching for the comfort of Pedro.

The rustling seemed to be getting closer.

"Maybe it's a rabbit?" Whispered Violet hopefully. The rustling continued to get louder until Violet let out a little shriek and jumped off the stump. We quickly drew together in fear. We waited, hardly daring to breath. It sounded as though whatever was coming had arrived. My heart was beating so hard it hurt and I was sure that if I looked down, I would have been able to see it moving beneath my sweatshirt.

I let out a small, involuntary moan and felt Amelia grasp my hand. As one, we took a deep breath and prepared for the horror that was coming. With a final rustle and a visible shake of the bush in front of us, out came... a rat. A massive, disgusting, worm-tailed, brown rat with horribly matted fur. It scurried out and across the path almost running its razor-sharp claws across my foot. I screamed and jumped about flapping my hands.

"Oh my god, oh my god, oh my god!" I squealed over and over, still jumping and flapping. "I HATE RATS! Urgh!" With one final shudder, I calmed and was able to think rationally and sensibly again. Everyone was staring at me, Amelia with a slight smirk on her face.

"I never knew you were afraid of rats!" She giggled at me. I scowled in response.

Violet let out a loud breath of relief and flopped back onto the tree stump from where she had fled just moments ago. Her bottom had barely touched the stump when she leapt up again with a loud yelp, hand clasped over her bottom; poor Titch had to let out a line of thread to stop himself hitting the floor as he was launched from her shoulder.

"What happened!?" asked Amelia, reaching out a caring hand to support her friend. Instead of answering though, Violet was bent over looking at the top of the stump where she had tried to sit down. She was running her hand over it and I heard her mutter, "That was definitely not there when I sat down earlier."

"What wasn't there?" I asked tentatively, slightly worried at my friend's strange behaviour.

"That," she replied, pointing. "That trail of holly. It wasn't there when I first sat down but the second time it was and it spiked my bum." She turned round to look at us, a confused expression distorting her face.

Amelia and I exchanged a brief glance before I gently said, "Violet it can't have just appeared. Maybe you sat further back when you sat down the second time?"

"No, I sat in the same place because I felt that knobbly bit there digging into my leg both times. I definitely…" She trailed off, slightly shaking her head. "Or maybe not. I don't know. Yeh, maybe I did sit differently." She absentmindedly rubbed her prickled bottom again and then said, "Shall we carry on?"

We all agreed and set off once again up the stony path. The busyness and excitement of the last few minutes had done a good job of warming us up a bit, so we started feeling slightly more comfortable and jollier. For a few minutes Amelia and I enjoyed laughing about my reaction to the horrid rat and even Violet shared a giggle. However, the gloom and chill soon crept in on us and we descended into quiet. After some time, our silence was, once more, shattered by a shriek from Violet.

"Ouch! Flipping holly again! Where did that come from?" she groaned, looking around.

"Violet, we're in a forest. I'm not sure why you're surprised by a bit of holly. Walk more in the centre of the path. You made me jump." Amelia responded bluntly.

I dropped back a pace or two to allow Violet more room as we carried on.

After a few more minutes of trudging, it was Amelia's turn to let out a gasp of pain.

"Argh, ow." She was rubbing her left arm just above her elbow.

"Holly?" asked Violet innocently, with a raise of one eyebrow.

"Actually, it was," replied Amelia with a slight frown. I saw a small smirk flit across Violet's face.

After a short moment, I shrieked, "OUCH! Oh for goodness sake. How have we all been prickled by holly?!" I laughed, rubbing my thigh where I had caught myself.

We shared a chuckle and carried on. It wasn't long before I noticed that the walls of green bordering the path were moving closer together.

"Ow!" yelped Amelia again closely followed by a call of, "Ouch!" from Violet. I myself was prickled again and it wasn't long before Pedro and Piggins had felt the holly leaves puncture their skin too. Even Titch let out a high-pitched shriek. After Pedro had neighed in pain, I glanced back to see if he was OK and was taken aback by what I saw.

"Hey, wait a sec," I called to the others. "I swear I just saw that holly branch move backwards off the path and into the hedge!"

"Now who's imagining things?" retorted Violet.

"No, I swear it did." I threw back. Amelia just rolled her eyes. She carried on walking but had barely gone more than a handful of steps before she stopped. I watched in horror as I saw an arm of holly whip out of the bush, jab Amelia in the neck and then snap back into the greenery like a lizard withdrawing its tongue. She squealed and spun around, just as another branch came at Violet from the other side of the path, getting her in the back of the knee. Almost instantly, a tongue of spikey dark green leaves shot out and drew a spot of blood from the back of my hand.

"What is going on?" I yelled, as, all of a sudden, vines of pin-sharp holly leaves were vaulting out of the hedges from both sides, jabbing at us wherever they could land a shot.

"Run!" bellowed Amelia. We didn't need telling twice. We set off at full speed up the path trying to duck and twist out of the reach of the holly. But the faster we ran the quicker we were attacked. The plants snaked towards us, ripping at our clothes and skin, until it had completely surrounded us in a thick prison of deadly leaves, hell bent on causing us as much pain as possible. The green canopy of the tree tunnel we had been walking down was now completely blocked out because they holly had surrounded us, holding us in its horribly sharp belly. I could feel the cruel leaves pulling at my hair, scratching at my face and hands, stinging with every new attack.

"This must be one of Thomas's traps!" Violet managed to shout in between shrieks of pain.

I agreed but couldn't say so as I was too busy trying to make myself as small as possible by curling up in a ball trying to protect as much of myself as I could.

Suddenly, a tiny voice shrieked in my ear; "Get ready to run!" It was Titch. I just about managed to nod in acknowledgement.

I waited, terrified, curled up in my ball, for whatever Titch was going to do. I didn't have to wait long. Finally there was a break in the painful jabbing and I felt Violet grab my shredded arm to pull me up the path. I sprang up and ran after her as fast as I could.

(She's a national sprinting champion so she's hard to keep up with!) I glanced back and could see Titch flying through the air, weaving bright webs around the darting plants trapping them, restricting their movement. We pounded up the path, Piggins flying alongside us and Pedro at full gallop behind. I was breathing hard and fast now, my legs and chest burning.

"TITCH!" I heard Amelia call, "COME ON!"

My body was starting to feel like it was going to give up but I was spurred on by the sight of a bright clearing up ahead. With one final surge of painful effort, I pushed my body after Violet and, finally, we reached the clearing and collapsed in a panting, sweaty heap. Piggins landed next to Amelia and Pedro flopped down next to me.

"Where's Titch?" panted Violet between harsh breaths.

"Is he not with you? He's always on your shoulder, isn't he?" I wheezed back.

"Did you not see what he did?" asked Piggins, a note of surprise in his grunty voice.

"What do you mean? He just told me to be ready to

run and then Violet grabbed me, and we ran," Amelia replied, her breathing coming slightly easier now.

"He span a web at the most incredible speed I've ever seen. He trapped all the holly in a huge web so that we could run. I... I don't think he was able to escape though." There was a silence filled with both tension and sadness at the thought of losing Titch.

"I saw him too. It was amazing. He was flying around trapping all the holly plants so we could run. But I thought he'd follow us once he was done," I added.

"So... so you're saying he sacrificed himself so we could escape?" asked Violet in a small voice.

"Umm yeh, that's what it looked like. I'm so sorry Violet." Piggins laid a pink trotter on Violet's hand. Amelia and I scooted over to hug our friend.

"But he was my Bond." She sniffed. "He's been whispering in my ear ever since I met him. Giving me confidence and support and... and stuff. I don't think I would have been able to get this far without him. He really understood my anxiety. Like no one ever has before." A trickle of tears mingled with the sweat on Violet's face and ran a race down to her chin before dropping onto the bright grass below.

We sat in silence, holding each other, each of us feeling the sadness and pain from the loss of Titch. The horror of the trap that Prince Thomas had laid, and the fear of what was to come next weighed heavily on our minds as our breathing slowly returned to normal.

Chapter 11

We lost track of how long we sat there, lost in thought. Eventually we became aware of a strange sound floating on the warm breeze. We looked around to find its source, Pedro's ears flicking back and forth listening hard. My heart immediately started beating faster in apprehension of another surprise attack. The noise seemed to be coming at us at quite a speed; we leapt to our feet, standing back to back in a circle as though preparing to fight, our breathing more rapid.

As whatever it was came closer, we were able to distinguish a pattern in the sound: it was a rhythmic beating like wings, and it seemed to be coming from the path we had so narrowly escaped from.

We huddled together, eyes glued to the path (which now looked innocently calm and peaceful). There, flapping through the trees was a bat. It was bobbing slightly in the air as its wings beat, flying towards us.

We were on the verge of turning to run again when the bat called out; "Violet?"

Violet's jaw dropped in surprise. "Yes?" she replied nervously.

The bat flapped over and hovered in front of her face, still bobbing up and down.

"I saw what happened back there, I hope you're ok." The bat spoke to Violet in a gentle voice. "I saw the spider weaving the web to save you. If he hadn't done that, there was no way you were getting out of there. I saw you all running out of the holly and the spider stayed behind holding the bush that was attacking you. As he'd saved you, I guessed he must be important to you so I saved him." The purply-black bat held open her little hands and there, safely clutched in her fur, was Titch. All his eyes were closed but you could just about see the rise and fall of his little chest.

A tear of happiness and relief rolled from Violet's eye as she gently took Titch and put him to her lips. He fluttered his eyes and a lazy smile spread across his little face.

"Thank you," she whispered to him before gently placing him in her pocket to keep him safe.

She looked back up at the bat, still hovering, and carefully pulled the bat into a warm embrace. The bat wrapped its dark blue wings around her and there was a moment of stillness. Amelia and I gasped as we saw the whisper of a rainbow flow around the pair.

"Another Bond!" I breathed to Amelia, unwilling to ruin this special moment.

Eventually, Violet held the bat in front of her at and smiled at it.

"I'm Plum." The bat smiled back.

The moment was broken by a little cough from Pedro. "Sorry to ruin the moment but we really need to get going. There's another spot of scales over there." He pointed to the start of yet another path, indicating which way we needed to go.

"Ready?" I asked. They all nodded, so we set off. This path was just mud with little patches of grass and moss. It was still surrounded by forest, but the canopy overhead was thinner and less spooky.

It was a nice walk and we chatted with each other, explaining to our Bonds what our home life was like.

"So does time stop whilst we're here then?" asked Amelia. She really wanted to be right about that.

"No," replied Pedro. "I forgot to explain that bit, didn't I? When you came through the door, a double was made of each of you. That double will be acting as you. It will think like you, talk like you, move like you. Well almost. It will do all of those things but not quite as *properly* as you."

"Won't our parents notice?" I asked in awe. The thought of a me-but-not-me living in my house was rather uncomfortable.

"The doubles won't feel very well, and your parents will be able to see that something isn't quite right. Just as when you are poorly, they will be sent to bed to recover. When you go back through the door, you will resume your lives and the doubles will vanish."

There was a pause as this information sank in.

"That's actually really clever. So, they'll never know we've been gone?" Violet asked.

"Yup. It's a well thought out piece of magic actually," Pedro replied.

"I really thought time would stop. You know, like in the story when the children go through to Narnia? That would have been a good idea too." Amelia so liked being right.

Further up the path, the trees that hid the sky thinned out and the sun was able to shine down on us, heating our cool limbs. The green of the surrounding plants shone vividly and we soon breathed more easily. As we turned a corner, the path levelled out and disappeared behind a wall of tangled hanging creepers. We all stopped and stared, each of us thinking that those creepers must definitely be another of Prince Thomas's traps or tricks.

"We have to go on. They're only thin, look. You can see the light from the other side through the gaps. It can't be that bad." Amelia said, although a faint quiver betrayed her confidence.

"But what if they wrap us up and don't let us go or something?" questioned Violet nervously.

"We don't really have a choice though. We must carry on. We must rescue the Princess. Maybe we should go through one at a time? That way, if something happens, those of us left behind can think of… something else," I finished, lamely.

"I'll go." Piggins volunteered. Nobody objected and so we approached the curtain of vines. Amelia bent down and grasped Piggins in a tight hug.

We waited and watched; breath held. Piggins took a deep breath, jutted his chin out and walked bravely into the creepers.

<u>Chapter 12</u>

"It's ok!" we heard him call from the other side, and we let out a huge sigh of relief. "You can follow me through! There is the most incredible plant over here." He sounded quite excited.

We pushed through the hanging sheet of vines and came out in a long clearing wide enough for two cars to pass but no more than that.

This time, instead of thick trees surrounding us there were steep, high walls of rock that even the best climber would have struggled to scale. The floor of the clearing was covered in grass and the strangest plants you've ever seen.

They were about as tall as our knees, with two rounded, grey-green leaves sticking out of the sides of brown stems. On top, sat a lurid pink bulbous head with a sprout of green leaves like hair.

None of us had ever seen plants like this and we each went to inspect one. The head of the plant was a sort of pear shape with hair on the large, rounded end. As it lifted its head, a wide round mouth opened at the thin end. I was astounded to see two eyes open and peer at me. Small bubbles were being blown from the mouth.

I looked around at my friends and saw that each plant was now blowing tiny bubbles. We raced through the clearing joyfully as more and more plants blew colourful bubbles into the air. We were laughing and giggling, running all over the place. The plants seemed to be waking up; they were starting to dance about on their stems, broad leaves waving around. The more they danced, the bigger the bubbles seemed to become until the air was shimmering with pink, blue and purple bubbles floating up towards the bright sky.

"Shh!" instructed Amelia. "Listen." So we did. Each time a bubble was released there was a small popping sound; the clearing was alive with the sound of POP POP POP.

"This is amazing!" I laughed, watching the bubbles drift lazily up and away from us.

"Ooo!" shivered Violet. "Have you popped one? It kind of fizzes."

We popped bubbles, enjoying the fizzy feeling that

whizzed up our arms. However, after I had popped about seven bubbles, my finger started to feel numb and I could no longer move it. I could see my friends inspecting their fingers too. The plants were now spewing out huge bubbles at a much faster rate, and the fizz from the big bubbles was considerably more than that from the small ones. Popping the giant bubbles brought on the feeling of numbness much sooner, and it wasn't long before I had three numb fingers and was starting to become quite worried.

"Lacey! Stop touching the bubbles!" shouted Violet. I looked at her and was horrified to see that her right arm was hanging by her side and she was limping. Pedro's tail was immobile, and his rear right leg was dragging. I jogged over to Violet and Amelia and felt my right arm go completely numb as an enormous bubble popped on my elbow. It flapped uselessly at my side as I came to a stop by my friends.

"Are you alright Amelia?" I asked. Her face looked weird.

"I caaa taall." she tried to reply, a frown scrunching her eyebrows and tears in her eyes.

"She popped a massive bubble with her tongue."

explained Piggins. If my friend hadn't been crying, I might have laughed.

"Is the numbness wearing off?" I asked.

Everyone shook their heads.

"Me neither. This must be another of Prince Thomas's traps." We stared out over the clearing; it was thick with enormous bubbles, deceptively beautiful in the sunlight.

As we stood staring, bubbles popped: on my cheek and I could feel dribble run down my chin as I couldn't hold my mouth closed; on Violet's right foot who then nearly fell over; Amelia's left arm; Pedro's ears, which flopped down either side of his face, and Plum's left wing that caused her to fall out of the air. Thankfully she landed safely on Violet's good arm.

I tried to shout to the others that we needed to get out of there, but my mouth just wouldn't work. It came out as a line of dribble and I stamped my foot in frustration, tears pricking my eyes. Thankfully, we all seemed to be having the same thought and started to move towards the opposite end of the clearing. It was hopeless though. Dancing flowers were throwing out bubbles so fast we could barely see clearly. We ran, as best we could, down the clearing but the bubbles just kept coming for us. Finger by finger, limb by limb we were going numb, barely able to keep moving. Eventually it was too much. We lay on the ground, keeping as low as possible to get away from the bubbles. Piggins tried crawling but a bubble made his bottom go numb.

"Ok, I have a plan," uttered Piggins. "I can fly high and fast. I will fly above you and beat my wings fast enough to clear a path in the bubbles. That will give you a clear run to the exit – it's not far."

"But if the bubbles touch you, you'll go numb too. If you fall you'll hurt yourself. What if a bubble numbs your wing?" Violet asked urgently. I could see the fear for Amelia's Bond etched on her face.

"I know it's a risk and I don't want to leave you, especially you Amelia, but I have to do this. It's your only way out. I'll be fine." He gave a brave smile before crouching down, ready to spring. "Are you ready?" he shouted. "Get ready to RUN!" We readied ourselves as best we could and waited for our cue. It came in a glorious flurry of beautiful feathers. Piggins shot upwards like a well-timed bullet through a gap in the bubbles. He angled his body and beat his wings hard and fast; even though the plants were working hard to produce bubbles, Piggins' wings blasted them away creating a clear path for us. We had to help each other move due to numb legs and feet, but together we stayed strong and half ran half limped our way along. Piggins was yelling from above: "Keep going! Hurry, hurry! You're nearly there." Finally, the edge of the clearing was only steps away and we tumbled, as a big bundle, clear of the hellish bubbles. As I rolled through the grass I heard a squeal and a loud thump. I looked back and was distraught to see Piggins lying on the ground, eyes closed, wings twisted at an odd angle. I barely thought for more than a second. I crawled back towards the bubbles once more, determined to rescue our fallen comrade. I reached out my good arm and grabbed hold of Piggins' trotter, dragged him towards me and rolled away from the danger, pulling Piggins over me as I went.

I heard Amelia cry out in horror when she saw Piggins lying still and twisted on the ground. I looked at her, desperate to say I was sorry but unable to because my mouth still wouldn't work.

We lay out of reach of the bubbles, but we had no energy to move on any further. We were a broken group and, as a wash of dizziness crashed over me, I fainted.

<u>Chapter 13</u>

I blinked my heavy eyes as I came round. My body felt weird and alien. It seemed that the bubbles' poison had spread through my body leaving me completely unable to move. My sight was fuzzy and I could only make out vague colours and blurry shapes.

Being stuck like this in an unknown world was terrifying but there was nothing I could do, so I used deep breathing (that I'd learnt at school) to try and calm myself down, and waited for my eyes to return to normal.

I became dimly aware of something moving near me. Given what we had already encountered that day, the thought of something else unknown near me filled me with dread. 'Please let it be Pedro.' I silently begged.

Without warning, a tiny face with bright green eyes peered down at me from above.

My fear must have shown because whoever the face belonged to spoke in a gentle, soothing voice: "My name is Blossom. It's ok. There is no need to be afraid. You are safe. I am here to help you."

It's all very well telling me not to be afraid, but when you're on a perilous journey, your body isn't working and a strange face appears, it's kind of hard not to.

"Shh, shh." the stranger said, stroking my hair with what felt like impossibly small hands. My heart was pounding but before you could say Help! the face had disappeared and I was left alone again, wondering whether I had imagined it.

My heart was just beginning to slow, when I felt the tiny hand against my hair again. It was lifting my head and I felt a rock being pushed under it, like a pillow. There was another pause and then I saw that the face belonged to a beautiful little fairy. I was amazed!

Blossom had a halo of bright yellow hair plaited around her head with five flowers nestled in it like a crown. She wore a stripy green top that sprouted gorgeous orange and yellow petals to form a skirt. Her long, dainty legs were tipped with sparkling bright pink ballet shoes, and a stunning pair of wings flapped effortlessly, keeping her airborne so I could see her. Her tiny, delicate hands held a roughly hewn wooden bowl in which sloshed a sparkling purple liquid.

She gently opened my mouth to pour the liquid in, but I moaned my reluctance; was this a minion of Prince Thomas trying to finish me off? With my body paralysed though, I was unable to do anything except watch as the fairy put the bowl to my lips and gently tip the fluid down my unwilling throat.

My frightened gaze held her calm one as I felt the coldness of the liquid trickle down into my tummy. As cold as it had been in my throat, it spread a delicious warmth through every fibre of my body, making it tingle and shiver. Shiver! I could shiver! My body was slowly coming back to me! I could feel my fingers and toes flexing, feel my legs twitching. I could move! I gingerly sat up and stretched my arms up to the sky, wriggling my fingers as I did so.

I turned and grinned at the fairy, which was still hovering next to me, a smile on her pretty face.

"Thank you!" I beamed at her, confident now that she was not sent by Prince Thomas. My face fell however as I saw my friends around me, still as statues on the grass.

"Come." Blossom beckoned to me. "We can bring

them round together. It will be quicker with two of us." I followed her a short distance to a peculiar tree. It was a hollowed-out stump with a pool of the purple liquid at the bottom. The tree stump had sprouted a new tree from the back of the hollow. The little tree stood proud, like a guard which, I suppose, it was, protecting the magic liquid it held at its roots.

Blossom handed me another small bowl and together we worked over the next few minutes ferrying liquid to my friends to revive them. One by one, they woke and stretched as I had, thrilled to be able to move once more. Squeals of joy soon filled the air as we hugged and exchanged smiles of gratitude with the fairy.

It took me a few minutes to realise that, even though we had revived Amelia, she wasn't jumping for joy with the rest of us. I looked around and felt my heart sink to my stomach as I saw her kneeling on the grass with Piggins cradled in her arms.

I walked over and knelt beside her. She looked at me with tears streaming silently down her face soaking the neck of her t-shirt.

"He's been revived. He is breathing and he has murmured but he won't fully wake up. Look at the state of his wings. Look what happened to him as he saved us." Amelia's voice cracked as she finished speaking and she started sobbing, her body heaving with sorrow.

"I'm so sorry Amelia." And I wrapped my arms around her. Soon we felt Violet join us, shortly followed by Pedro.

"He was in a bad way when I found you," Blossom explained. "I have done what I can. He will come round but it will take time. Love him and care for him and he will be fine." She smiled at Amelia, who returned a look of hope.

"Thank you," she whispered to the fairy. "Thank you."

"You are welcome, all of you. Now, you must go. You need to continue your journey to Prince Thomas's hideaway. Follow that path and be careful." She pointed to one of several paths leading away from where we were.

"Can't you come with us?" Violet asked.

"No, I must stay here; the forest needs me. I am sorry. Now go." And she fluttered around us, herding us like sheep towards the path that she had pointed to.

"Thank you!" I called over my shoulder one last time

before turning and following my friends, glad and relieved to spot yet another shimmer of mermaid scales.

<u>Chapter 14</u>

This time the climb along the path was much steeper, windier and tougher. It wasn't long before we were panting and sweating with the effort, although none of us as much as Amelia who was also carrying Piggins.

There was a break in the surrounding foliage, and I paused briefly to look through the gap. Far below, winking in the sun, was the sea, the white tops of the waves barely visible from this height. Straight below us was never-ending forest stretching right down to the edge of the glistening sandy beaches. Every now and then, a colourful bird would swoop out of the treetops only to dive back in as though playing a game.

When I looked up the mountain, I was alarmed to see just how close we were to the mouth of the volcano. I knew it was extinct, but the black rock and thick vegetation was eerie, silhouetted against the bright sky.

We stopped for another break. Jumpers were stripped off. Piggins was gently lain on the floor so Amelia could shake off the soreness in her arms and Pedro hunted out some juicy leaves so we could all take in a little water (although it wasn't really enough). Together, we used our excess clothing to create a sling for Amelia to carry Piggins in; there was no way she could go much further with his weight in her arms.

We moved off once more along the path that was damp and muddy, but before long I realised that the dirt under our feet was becoming drier and cracked, like mud in a field that hasn't had rain for weeks. The trees surrounding us had once borne colourful flowers but now these were blackened and dried out; ugly, dark skeletons.

"Can you hear that?" Violet asked, as we all became aware of an eerie sound echoing down the volcano towards us. "I don't like it." She slowed down to walk closer to me, seeking comfort.

"It's just the wind. Come on, we must be nearly there now. There's not much of this mountain volcano thing left for us to climb!" Amelia puffed.

But it wasn't just the wind. It carried with it what sounded like hundreds of high-pitched moaning voices, whispering threats of our deepest fears if we continued to travel the path.

I shook my head, trying to rid my brain of the images being planted there, and squeezed my eyes shut against the horror. It was too much though and I fell to my knees, sobbing, hands over my ears trying to block out the voices.

Not far up ahead I could see Violet curled in a ball around Plum on the dusty ground, great sobs shaking her body. Pedro sat in front of me, glistening tears rolling down his pearly-white face, his proud unicorn horn becoming dull the more he wept.

The voices on the wind were now swirling around us in a torrent of dust snatched from the ground, whipping at our hair, and pulling at our clothes. I foolishly opened my eyes for mere moments, only to feel them filled with flying dirt.

I felt my heart was breaking as my greatest fears played over and over in my mind, intensified by the tornado pinning us down. Somehow, over the racket surrounding me, I heard the thundering of feet, felt strong hands under my arms, lifting me to standing. I sheltered my eyes so I was able to open them a crack and see who was helping. In front of me stood the determined face of Amelia. She had an aura of pale light pulsing around her and seemed unaffected by the howling winds. As though from far away, I heard her shouting: "Come on Lacey, you need to move. Just think of positive things, don't let it get into your head." She put her warm hands on my face and used her thumbs to wipe away my tears. "You can do this! Fight it! We must keep going." I nodded at her, spurred on by her strength. She grasped my hand and dragged me towards Violet. I pulled Pedro along with my other hand and, together, we heaved Violet and Plum off the floor. Her face was streaked with dirt, tears snaking tracks down her face. Amelia spoke firmly to Violet as she had to me and then grabbed us both, one hand each, and pulled us forward, up and up the path with the tornado still swirling around us. The harder she pulled us along, the stronger the light around her became as though her strength was fuelling it. This beacon of light was all I focused on as we stumbled up the path.

And suddenly, as though hit by an invisible wall, the voices quietened, the wind stilled, the dust settled. The light around Amelia dimmed, and we were able to stand, gasping, reining in our ragged breath.

"How did you…?" I stuttered at Amelia. "What… light… how?"

"I just kept thinking of positive things rather than letting those evil voices get into my head. I fought back and the harder I fought, the stronger I felt. I guess it made me just strong enough to block it all out and help you guys."

"Just like Queen Beatrice said." breathed Violet. "She said your positivity would help us! Well done Amelia. Thank you!"

Looking around, we saw that we had reached the top. The path had opened out onto a flat plateau of hard stone surrounded by rock rather than trees, and along the ground was one long dried up trail of mermaid scales leading to a dead end at the rock-face.

We raced over and began patting different parts of the wall trying to find a way in. I felt a cold breeze nip at my cheeks, and I knew I'd found something.

"Over here!" I exclaimed. "There's a crack. Let's try pushing it together." We put all our weight against the solid wall and heaved. With a great echoing, grinding moan, a chunk of rock swung inwards to reveal a passageway.

Chapter 15

We shuddered as a blast of icy air shot up the passageway to greet us. We just had time to see a sandy floor and rough walls cut from the rock with splashes of mermaid scales disappearing into the gloom beyond. Along the walls were candle holders but no light came from them. The door slammed shut behind us and we were plunged into thick inky blackness, the type where you can't tell if your eyes are open or closed.

"Well we know she's been here, so we'll just have to go carefully and keep going." Amelia murmured into the freezing dark space.

"Wait!" came Plum's voice. "I'll go first. I can use echolocation to guide us along. Violet - hold my leg and the rest of you make a train behind. Don't let go!" Obediently, we all grabbed hold of each other and waited for our line to move off.

It was a slow and cold journey as Plum confidently led us through a labyrinth of passages: some flat, some uphill, some down.

The line came to an abrupt stop and we all crashed into the back of each other with a chorus of groans and squeals.

"What's the problem? Are we lost?" called Pedro from the back.

"No," quivered Plum's voice in return. "There's a hole in the floor that you're going to have to jump over."

This statement was met with a stony silence. I shivered, not just from the bitter cold, as I considered how we were to jump successfully over a hole we couldn't see. How would we know how far to jump? I'm not scared of heights, but I'm scared of falling and the thought of plummeting through blackness into who-knew-what, was terrifying.

"How are we supposed to jump over a hole we can't see?" snapped Violet, reading my mind, her teeth chattering. "We'll fall."

I leant against the cold, damp wall and worried a fingernail with my teeth. I thought back over all that we had achieved since stepping through the door from my bedroom. I pictured the grief on the Queen's face when she'd told us what had happened to her daughter.

I recalled Titch's bravery when he had used his webs to hold off the attacking holly. I felt a fresh wave of sorrow at the thought of Piggins tumbling from the air after helping us through the poisonous bubbles. The numbness, the fairy that had helped us so we could carry on our journey and Amelia, glowing as her positivity guided us through the latest horror. We had already come through so much, stayed so strong; we couldn't turn back now or everything that we had done would have been for nothing.

I pushed off the wall and, in a voice stronger than I felt, said, "I'll go first. Once I'm over, Plum are you strong enough to carry Piggins over to me? That way, Amelia will be able to jump more safely. Pedro, can you jump or do you need Plum as well?"

"Lacey, you can't! What if you fall? We don't know how far you'll go, where you'll end up or even whether you'll survive." Violet's voice wobbled. "Let's turn back. We can't jump, it's just too risky."

"Violet, we have to. Think of everything we've done since we arrived here. Think of the Queen and the Princess. We *can't* turn back now." I argued back.

"But…" began Violet. I didn't give her a chance to

finish. I knew if I thought about it any longer, I wouldn't find the courage to do it. Before I could second-guess myself, I ran blindly into the thick darkness. As soon as I felt Plum's wing brush my cheek, I jumped. The fear, worry, pain and horrors of the day flashed through my mind, fuelling my body to launch, stretch, fly through the darkness, over the unknown depths below me. I felt the top of my head brush the dripping ceiling, was vaguely aware of my boot slipping (but thankfully just about clinging on), and felt the cold air burning my throat, as it passed through my wide open mouth which was held in a silent scream.

I landed painfully but safely on the other side of the hole. Sitting down, back against the wall, I felt sick with relief. I was unable to confirm my safety for a few moments, whilst I gathered my thoughts and calmed myself.

"I'm ok!" I finally managed to call, slapping a hand over my mouth to supress an anxiety burp. I pushed myself up and winced as the pain in my ankle shot up my leg.

"How big was the jump?" Amelia's voice echoed

loudly through the blackness.

"I have no idea." I called back. "I just jumped as far as I could. Just go for it. It can't be that far; we all know how much better I am at maths than PE!" I heard a weak giggle from the other side and rolled my eyes despite my smile.

"Amelia, let's get Piggins over first. Plum, can you do that?" I waited patiently through the scuffling and muttering that I took to be the others transferring the little pig from Amelia to Plum. After a fluttering of leathery wings, I felt Plum land heavily at my feet. I bent down and, as gently as I could, lifted the warm soft body of the pig into my arms.

I limped him away further down the passage to give my fellow jumpers plenty of landing space. One by one, I heard the thunder of running feet, the whoosh of a flying body, and the thump of a landing. Lastly, came the rapid clip-clopping of unicorn hooves and the resounding clatter of Pedro landing.

We paused in the penetrating darkness, silently congratulating ourselves on successfully conquering the fall of doom, each one of us quietly grateful to have made it over safely.

I groped through the dark searching for Amelia so I could pass Piggins back to her. I felt confident that he would heal quicker if he was close to his Bond. I helped my friend re-attach him to her body using our jumpers. We could have used our clothing to help keep off the damp chill but, without needing to voice it, we knew that keeping Piggins safe was far more important than how cold we were.

All settled and ready to continue, we reassembled our train behind Plum and blindly followed the bat down the never-ending maze, trusting that she would safely guide us to wherever we needed to be.

Finally, finally we slowed to a stop as we caught a glimpse of a dim light up ahead. Now, just able to see each other's faces, we held our hands to our lips to signal to be quiet.

We pressed ourselves to the cold rock walls to avoid being seen and crept, as quietly as we could, towards the flickering light. As we approached, a ghastly voice drifted towards us although we could not hear the words clearly. We continued to creep, ninja-like, towards the voice until we found ourselves on the edge of an opening that looked down into a spacious, dimly-lit cavern.

<u>Chapter 16</u>

Torches danced on the walls casting eerie shadows where the rock walls were uneven and jagged, and, down below, pacing around the floor of the echoing chamber was a tall, slender man. His head was completely bald except for a horseshoe of dark, scruffy hair. Long, thin, gnarled fingers clasped together behind his slightly stooped back and he was talking to a creature none of us could ever have imagined, not even in our darkest nightmares.

It had the strong, shaggy back legs of a great grizzly bear with huge dinner plate-sized paws.

The body of a tiger with dirty fur and poisonous-green scales covered grossly oversized lizard-like front legs with razor sharp claws. And, finally, the head of a Hellhound dog with matted black fur wrapping a huge skull. Staring red eyes glowed from sockets sunk deep in the filthy hair and yellow stained dagger teeth stood proud in its open jaw, dripping foul saliva onto the dank floor.

"The Queen is still not willing to hand over the throne to me," sulked the man, confirming that this was, indeed, Prince Thomas.

"Master, we have had the daughter for some time now. Perhaps it is time to show the Queen how far we are willing to go?" The beast responded with a loud, low growling voice that vibrated right through to my core. It made me shiver and the hairs on the back of my neck stood on end.

The cruel Prince continued to pace as though considering what his vile companion had suggested, whilst the creature frowned at his master, awaiting a reply.

Abruptly, the pacing stopped, and Prince Thomas turned to face his beast. We cowered, terrified, in the shadows, aware that if the Prince were to cast his glance upwards, he would see several pairs of eyes watching him and our quest would be over. The floor was damp and freezing cold underfoot, and I felt Violet start to shiver, but the fear of detection kept us firmly rooted to the spot.

"Yes. Perhaps you are right. I really thought the mere kidnap would be enough. The world over knows how much she has treasured her daughter since the loss of the father." Prince Thomas scowled and began to pace again, his black shoes slapping against the wet floor.

We waited with bated breath, hoping for some sign or signal as to where the Princess was being held. We could go no further with our mission without knowing where she was.

As quietly as was physically possible, Plum muttered, "Shall I go off and try to find where Isla is being hidden? If we can get to her before they create a plan, we might have a better chance of rescuing her and getting her home."

We crawled backwards into the dark tunnel. A whispered conversation followed. The general thought was that this was, indeed, a good idea and so Plum, flying as close to the roof of the cavern as possible, disappeared off into the darkness in search of Isla.

Peering down once more at the cruel pair, we listened intently as the Prince continued his conversation with the creature.

"Your majesty, you have waited far longer than is reasonable. I strongly feel that it is now time to act." The creature bowed in respect as he finished, clearly afraid of being told off by its master for speaking out of turn.

"Malum, you faithful creature. You have waited so patiently. You are right. Go and fetch the revolting fish-creature and bring her to me. We will begin the next stage of my plan. I am fed up of waiting.

We will send the girl's crown to her pitiful Mother with a note to say the longer we wait, the more pieces we will send, starting with locks of her hair.

Then see how quickly she hands over the throne to me. If my plan continues to fail, Malum my loyal slave, then you will have your wish. I will allow you to sink your vile teeth deep into her flesh and enjoy the taste of a rare flavour."

Malum bared his foul teeth in a grin and licked his lips with a long, wet tongue. He bowed again, turned on his mismatched feet and stalked off down a corridor, a low growl rumbling deep in his throat. We watched a while longer and saw the Prince approach a stone table we had, until now, not noticed. We saw him pick up what looked like a roll of thick cellotape and then, to our horror, we saw him lift a long silver blade up to the light. The sharp edge glinted in the orange light and a wicked, thin smile spread over the Prince's ugly face.

I let out a gasp and Amelia slapped a wet, chilled hand across my mouth to stifle my sound of terror. She glared at me with wide eyes, mouthing SHUT UP at me. As one, we scurried back into the tunnel again for another muted conversation.

"What are we going to do?" breathed Violet, audibly shaken by what we had heard. "Plum needs to hurry."

"I don't know but we have to stay strong. Plum flies fast so I'm sure she will return soon. If she hasn't found Isla, we can tell her which corridor Malum headed down and she can go again." Amelia frantically whispered back.

We lay still, listening to the Prince's footsteps and watching the lights flickering around the cave, each silently begging for the rapid return of Plum.

Finally, the sound of flapping wings announced her arrival, and Violet welcomed her back with a warm embrace before allowing her to tell us the news.

"The good news is I found Princess Isla. She is being held in a shallow pool down one of the corridors. We must hurry though, that vile animal is nearly there."

"How do we get there?" I asked.

"This is the bad news. We will have to go through the cavern where Prince Thomas is."

"We know he's not going to leave because he's waiting for Malum to bring Isla to him. What are we going to do?" Violet uttered, her voice quivering.

"We're going to have to fight." announced Amelia. We all stared at her. "Don't look at me like that.

What choice do we have? If we go now, we will be able to tackle the Prince on his own, which will be easier than taking on both him and Malum at the same time."

"How, *how,* are we supposed to fight that… that thing?!" whimpered Violet. Amelia just stared at her and then said, "One thing at a time. We can do this. Remember, the spell chose us."

"Maybe, but did it know there would be this at the end?" Violet's voice was getting higher and shriller as her panic built.

"I don't know. But we're here and we have to at least try. Come on girls, we can do this." Amelia tried to give each of us a comforting smile, but it was a bit wobbly as her own worry broke through too.

"Amelia," I whispered. "We have to come back this way to get out. Why don't we leave Piggins here, wrapped up, so you don't have to carry him?"

"Good idea." she replied, and we worked together to untangle him from her body and lay him on the ground, as comfortably as we could.

"Ooo, I've got an idea!" Amelia suddenly lit up; eyes bright. "How about I go down first, pretend I'm on my own. Whilst I keep him occupied, you two sneak down to that table and grab the tape. Plum, you watch and as soon as they have the tape, swoop down and the flap around his head as close as you can to distract him."

"Whilst he's battling with Plum," I interrupted, "we'll bring the tape over and together we can take him down!" I finished, seeing the plan Amelia had concocted.

"Exactly." She nodded back.

"And the terrifying scary beast?" interjected Violet.

"One thing at a time! Let's just get that awful man down first." Amelia replied firmly.

My stomach churned as though a million enormous butterflies were fighting to escape. My mouth had gone so dry I could barely swallow, and my hands were practically dripping with sweat. My heart was beating painfully in my chest too, as if it wanted to leave along with the butterflies.

"Are we ready?" Amelia asked, her voice noticeably shaking.

"As ready as we'll ever be." I muttered under my breath, and with that, Amelia disappeared over the edge of the opening, into the cave and the dangers below.

<u>Chapter 17</u>

We heard her scrabbling down the slope and it wasn't long before the Prince noticed her descending the walls.

"Who the devil are you?!" he exclaimed, clearly taken utterly by surprise. "How did you get in here?"

We crawled around Piggins, back to the opening so we could watch and wait for our moment to come.

"Thought your traps and tricks were good, did you?" asked Amelia in a confident, cocky voice that totally betrayed the nerves she was feeling. "Which one was your best one, do you think?"

The Prince looked dumbstruck. "No-one should have been able to pass my spells. What magic do you possess?" he spat at Amelia.

"Magic? Me? Oh, wouldn't you like to know." I silently thanked Amelia's Mum for making her go to

Drama club every weekend; her ability to improvise was clearly coming in handy. "What would you like to know first? How we got past the death holly? The paralysing bubbles or perhaps the tornado of nightmares?"

I suddenly realised what Amelia was doing: as she was talking, she was, step by step, walking around the floor of the cave so that Prince Thomas's back was now towards us.

"Now's our chance!" I whispered to Violet. She screwed up her face before nodding once. We scrambled as carefully and quietly as we could. Thankfully, the wall was cut roughly into the rock so there were plenty of hand and footholds for us to use. We reached the safety of the floor and, crouching, ran towards the table. I picked up the tape and waved it towards the darkness of the opening we'd been hiding in, hoping that Plum would see my signal.

As quietly as I could, I whispered to Violet that the tape we had found was stuff my Dad used at home; "I think it's called duck tape, or something. It's crazy strong. If we manage it, we can wrap it around his hands and feet like they do in the movies. Maybe put one over his mouth too." She nodded back.

We stayed crouched down, hidden behind the table, listening to Amelia talking absolute rubbish at the Prince.

I had to hand it to her; she did a great job. Within a few short moments we saw Plum swoop gracefully out of the corridor and plummet, full speed, for Prince Thomas's head. He immediately started flapping and shrieking; this was our cue. We jumped up and sprinted towards Amelia.

Plum whipped around his head fast and furious, jabbing at him with her clawed feet. Frustratingly though, he was waving his arms around so wildly that we were unable to get close, and I took a sharp, stinging slap to the face. I stumbled backwards, hand held over my cheek and watched in despair as the Prince managed to just grab a handful of Plum's wing and launch her, full strength, at the cave wall. She hit it with a dull thud and slumped, unconscious, to the floor. "NOOOOO!" wailed Violet, starting to run towards her Bond, but I grabbed her and shouted to her that she could get him later because we needed her now.

Without the bat distracting him, Prince Thomas was able to see the full scale of the attack we had launched at him.

His face twisted in a grin as he laughed: "Children? She sends children to try and defeat me? She is more foolish than I thought. Perhaps she doesn't want her *precious* daughter back at all!" And with that, he lunged at Violet and grabbed her long hair, pulling her to the ground. She squealed as she went down but managed to twist and roll out of his grasp as Amelia landed a kick on his kneecap, making his leg give way beneath him. Howling in pain, he forced himself to stand and threw a wild fist at Amelia: his aim was true and she went sprawling backwards across the dirty floor.

From her position on the ground, Violet wrapped her slender arms around the man's ankles, holding on as tightly as she could. He tried to kick out but her athletic limbs held strong. He swung his arms wildly trying to maintain his balance, and he managed to crack another palm across my face: I could feel blood gush from my nose, which felt thick and painful.

"HURRY!" bellowed Violet from where she was still

grasping his legs with all her might.

I wiped my nose with the bottom of my t-shirt, crawled over to Amelia and dragged us both up. We ran, full pelt at Prince Thomas. Amelia collided with his body, which went crashing to the floor with an echoing crack. His fall seemed to have dazed him so we took full advantage of the few still moments. As quickly as I could, I wound the sticky black tape around his ankles, round and round and round, whilst Violet went up to help Amelia pin his upper body down. Once I was satisfied that enough layers of tape bound his legs, I span on my knees to face my friends. Violet was sitting firmly on the man's stomach and Amelia sat on his chest, holding his hands together ready for me to bind. I started to pass the tape around his wrists but the knock to his head was passing and he started to fight back, trying to separate his arms before it was too late. I shrieked to my friends for help: they appeared either side of me, each one holding a fighting arm, pushing his hands together so I could continue tying them up.

Panting, sweat dripping from our faces with the effort, the man was finally tied up and incapable of movement. He rolled his head fiercely from side to side and bucked his body like a flailing fish, trying to stop me slapping one last piece of tape across his mouth, but, working together, we finally had him taped up as best as we could make him.

Amelia and Violet lay back on the floor gasping, wiping the sweat from their dirty faces, but I knew we did not have a moment to spare. I urged my friends to get up so they could help me drag the prone man across the cave. We hid him behind the table and I tucked the dagger into my belt in case he somehow managed to get to it.

"We need somewhere to hide," I frantically suggested. We didn't want to be out in the open when Malum returned.

At that moment, we heard the tapping of his claws approaching and the dull whoosh of something being dragged along the floor. I dived behind the table, not taking much care if I trod on the Prince or not. Amelia followed me and we looked round for Violet, but realised she had gone the opposite way across the cave to find Plum. I peeped over the table and made eye contact with Violet. She was standing in wide-eyed fear, close to the entrance of the passageway Malum was coming down... she'd never make it back to us before he appeared in the cave.

Holding Plum, I saw her shrink back into the shadows as best she could as the terrible beast dragged the body of Princess Isla into view.

<u>Chapter 18</u>

We could see a glistening trail of water and scales being left behind in the dirt. Her beautiful tail was dirty and flapped feebly, and a wave of thick, long hair dragged along the cave floor collecting dried mud and dust. What should have been a beautiful gold crown sat grubby and askew on her head, and her long, tanned arms were scratched and bruised.

Malum dragged Princess Isla to the centre of the cave and stopped, sniffing the air.

"Master?" he growled into the seemingly empty room. Next to me, Prince Thomas strained against the tape and tried to call out but, mercifully, the piece across his mouth muffled his voice to almost silence. I glared at him and showed him the dagger in a silent threat. He frowned back at me, twitching his head in anger.

Still sniffing the air, Malum dropped the Princess on the floor and started to prowl through the dim cavern hunting for his master. I saw Violet breath out a sigh of relief as the great beast walked away from where she was cowering. Unfortunately, this meant that it was coming towards Amelia and me instead.

I could hear the clipping of its disgusting claws on the floor growing louder as it approached. My heart raced, my head buzzed, and the butterflies flew a whirlwind in my tummy. All sensible thought left me, and I was left with a primal instinct to survive. My fight or flight response kicked in as the grotesque animal got closer and, as his sniffing intensified showing that he could smell us, I rose like a wild lion and ran, screaming, towards him, dropping the knife as I did so. I had no idea what I was going to do but the sudden appearance of a screaming banshee startled Malum just long enough; I swung myself up onto his stripy back and dug my hands deep into its thick fur for something to grip onto.

He didn't remain frozen for long. Before I knew it, Malum was bucking and rearing trying to shake me off. I clung on with my hands and knees, as tight as I possibly could. I felt the rumble of his growls travelling through his body and up into mine. I had no idea how long I was going to be able to stay on the creature's back, nor what good it would do but I knew one thing: as long as Malum was distracted, he couldn't be hurting the Princess.

My hands and thighs were beginning to burn with the effort and my breath was coming so rapidly it was scratching my throat. Malum continued his efforts to rid himself of me but with another loud battle cry, Amelia came tearing out from behind the table, dagger raised in her hand. She swung out with the blade aiming for his face, but his reactions were quick. This time, as he reared up on his hind bear-like legs. I slipped and fell to the floor with a thwack. Dazed and bruised, I tried to roll away but before I could move, Malum's hot, stale breath fogged my face and I could feel drops of saliva splatter onto my forehead. I thought I was done for but suddenly the beast's head shot away from me with a great wail of agony and anger. It landed on its front lizard-legs and span around to stare at its behind. Sticking out of the thick fur was the handle of the knife. Whilst he was distracted, Amelia ran to me and pulled me away, stumbling as she did so. I clambered to my feet.

Shooting out of her hiding place, Violet joined us and together, we charged back towards the beast. Amelia went for his face, wildly swinging her fists. Violet went for his belly and I went for the knife. It took a great effort to yank the blade from his flesh but out it came bringing with it another howl of pain and a spurt of blood that soaked into my t-shirt.

Amelia was ducking and weaving, managing to avoid being struck by the sharp claws and strong jaws, at the same time aiming sharp blows at any part of his body she could reach. Violet was throwing kicks at the great stomach trying to weaken the animal as best she could. In a blur, Malum swung a great green leg at Amelia. It wiped her clean off her feet, sending her crashing into the mermaid. Continuing its sweep, the leg came round to throw Amelia hard into a wall, and then swept round again to meet me. I managed to dodge out of the way, but not before a clawed foot connected with my hand, sending the knife clattering away into the darkness.

The terrifying monstrosity faced me head on. It didn't swing or lunge, it didn't shoot out a clawed foot or try to take a bite. It merely glared at me, red eyes winking out of the gloom. It was as though it knew it had won.

It prowled slowly towards me, forcing me to walk backwards until I felt my back collide with the slimy wall. I was shaking from head to foot, my chest ached, and I was too scared to even blink. We had failed. After all we had been through, we had failed at the last hurdle. We had come so close to success. Princess Isla was right there. I could see her. Amelia and Violet were touching her, yet we couldn't beat this last obstacle.

"Take her and run!" I bellowed into the darkness to my two friends. "I'll keep him distracted whilst you two get the Princess back home."

"No!" came two voices back to me. "We're not leaving you."

"You have to. Just go." I called back, annoyed they weren't listening. "Just go!" I repeated, my voice breaking and tears starting to flow down my filthy face. Suddenly, out of nowhere, I felt the warm comforting softness of Pedro's fur against my palm.

I had completely forgotten about him. In a moment of clarity, I realised it must have been incredibly painful to see us battling and not be able to help due to the impossible task of climbing down the wall. Yet here he was, next to me, pouring strength and courage into me.

"Sorry I'm late." he muttered. "Had a little trouble getting down the wall. Not easy with hooves and no thumbs." Despite myself, I smiled. "What's the plan?" He asked out of the corner of his mouth.

"I've no idea." I whispered back, still not taking my eyes off Malam's.

"Right. Excellent." came Pedro's reply.

Suddenly, the beast pounced with jaws wide open, tongue lolling and claws stretching out to grab me. I screamed and dropped to my knees waiting for the piercing pain of his teeth to sink into me. But the pain didn't come. Instead, a shrill, awful howl filled the cave followed by an empty, echoing silence. I stayed on the floor, arms held protectively over my head for some time, waiting for something to happen. But nothing did. The silence stretched on and finally

I brought my arms down and pushed myself to my feet.

What I saw made me gasp. My hands shot to my mouth and my eyes stretched wide. My heart leapt to my throat and tears instantly prickled my eyes. Before was the slumped body of Malum. Not moving, not twitching, nothing. And sticking out from underneath his great hairy body was a little white leg with a sparkly blue hoof.

"No." I whispered into the silence. "No no no no no." I rushed over to try and pull the great lump off Pedro, but its weight felt like an elephant. I continued trying to push and pull the monster away and eventually I became aware of Amelia and Violet beside me. We spread out along the length of its body and, together, we heaved and pushed with all the remaining strength we could muster. Bit by bit, centimetre by centimetre, Pedro's little body became visible. With one final enormous shove, Malum rolled and we could at last get to the unicorn.

His horn had been snapped off deep in the belly of the beast. A glittering stump shone mystically from his forehead. I knelt and scooped my Bond up into my arms. I held him close to my chest and buried my face in his soft mane. A great wash of relief crashed over me as I felt his warm breath tickle my arm and I realised I could feel his heart beating against the palm of my hand. I glanced up and grinned at my friends through thick tears. They grinned back and them came to wrap us in a huge hug.

"As lovely as this is," announced Amelia, "We really should get out of here."

The three of us, me holding Pedro, stood and made our way to Princess Isla, who was lying utterly stunned on the floor. Violet dashed off and fetched Plum, then sat down next to me and Isla. Amelia said, "Back in a sec," and disappeared into the gloom. After a few minutes, we heard her scrabbling back down the rocks, followed by a thud which I took to be her kicking the still-tied-up Prince. She jogged over with Piggins gently wrapped in her strong arms and she, too, sat next to us on the floor.

"Is he still tied up?" I asked Amelia.

"Yup. He's not going anywhere. Whatever that tape is, it's incredibly strong. I suggest we don't hang around though. It might be worth calling for our ride home from here as we can't all get up the rock face." She said with a glance at Isla.

I frowned at Amelia, initially unsure as to what she was saying but then, with a jolt, I remembered the shell I had been given by Queen Beatrice. Without hesitation, I placed it against my lips and whispered that we were ready to go home. A small glow started to grow from within the shell; it grew and grew until it became a dazzling bright light that lit up the whole horrible cavern. It strained against the chain of the necklace as though trying to break free. I fumbled with the clasp and as soon as I had it open, the shell, surrounded by brilliant white light, shot off up the corridor we had come down, and away from us until we were left in the dark gloom once more.

Princess Isla still lay staring dumbly at us, so I took it upon myself to introduce ourselves and explain how we had come to be there. I recounted the whole story of what had happened since we sat down to watch the film at my house. She ooh'd and aah'd in all the right places and gasped at the really scary bits. I talked and talked until my voice grew hoarse, eventually arriving at the part of the story where she had come in.

Princess Isla's voice was soft; as she spoke it was filled with sadness. "You have been through all that danger just for me? Just to take me home?" Her gentle voice broke as she burst into shimmering tears.

"The spell chose us. We knew we'd been chosen for a reason. If we didn't help you, who would?" Amelia replied with a modest shrug.

The tears running down her face left clear trails and they continued to fall as the Princess manipulated her grubby tail so that she was able to sit up. Balancing carefully, she beckoned each of us towards her with open arms to give us each a huge hug. She whispered thank you to each of us and we sat, huddled together, waiting for help to arrive.

As we sat, she told us all about her world: about living as a Princess under the water, what it was like to have the Queen as your Mum and how she had lost her beloved Father. She then moved on to tell us how the wicked Prince had kidnapped her, where she'd been kept and how she knew what was going to happen if she didn't make it home.

"Our whole world was going to be ruled by that awful man. Imagine that! You've seen how beautiful it is here, how peaceful. It's unbearable to think what it would be like if someone so wicked and cruel were to be on the throne." The silence that followed as we all thought about what it would be like was punctuated by the moans, groans and shuffles of Prince Thomas, still tied up and stuck behind the stone table.

Still waiting for our rescue, the rush of what had happened wore off and the cold began to seep into our bones once more. The dirt, blood and grime that we were caked in was drying, making our skin uncomfortable and itchy. We had all started to shiver when finally, the cave grew lighter and we could hear a clattering and neighing sound approaching. The white light grew, and we stood up (apart from Isla!) to watch in wonder as our peculiar ride home arrived.

<u>Chapter 19</u>

Galloping through the air were two dazzling white, sparkling seahorses with glittering multicoloured tummies. Flowing behind them were their manes, one of gold, one of silver. I couldn't see how they were flying, assumed it was more wonderful magic, and stared in awe. As they flew gracefully through the air, they pulled with them a blanket of light, illuminating the cave, banishing all the darkness and horrors within. They halted before us looking grand and important and I saw, around the silver-maned seahorse, the shell that I had been given by Queen Beatrice.

"The Queen received your call for help; we came as quickly as we could. It wasn't easy to find you down here! Her Majesty eagerly awaits your return. Let us leave at once!" The shell around the seahorse's neck lifted into the air, slid off its head and hovered in front of us.

We waited, spellbound, watching as the shell began to grow bigger and bigger until it was so large, Father

Christmas could have used it for his deliveries!

Finally, it stopped growing and stood, glowing in the middle of the cave, silver runners resting on the floor in the dirt.

"Climb in then!" instructed the seahorses. We glanced at each other with excitement. We worked together to help Princess Isla into the shell sleigh and then clambered up to join her. Once we had settled our wounded Bonds gently into our laps, turquoise ropes wove their way from the sleigh to fix around the seahorses.

"How are we going to get out?" I whispered to Amelia. "This will never fit back down that passageway!"

"I have no idea." she whispered in return, with a shrug of her shoulders.

We didn't have to wait long for an answer, though. As the seahorses rose, pulling the sleigh behind them, the dark, rocky roof of the cave shimmered and suddenly completely disappeared!

"Wow!" we all breathed in amazement.

The sleigh continued to glide through the air, up and out through the top of the volcano into the bright blue sky. We had been in the dark for so long, the sun's brightness forced our eyes shut. However, I did not want to miss the spectacular view we would have of the world from this high up, so I squinted until I was able to open my eyes again. It was worth it. Far below, green trees and colourful flowers grew in abundance, reflecting the bright light. Ahead, the rich blue sea twinkled and danced, kissing the soft sand of the beaches. Bruises, bumps, cuts and scratches were forgotten as I gazed at the beauty, and a huge swell of peace and happiness ballooned in my chest. 'We did it." I thought to myself, a smile blossoming on my dirty, bruised face.

"Pardon?" Violet's voice broke into my bubble.

"What?" I asked back, confused.

"You said something." she said, also sounding confused.

"Did I? Oh!" I laughed, "I didn't realise I'd said it out loud! I was just thinking… we did it! We actually did it. Look! We are all here, safe. And Princess Isla is with us too." I beamed happily.

I looked over at the Princess who was sitting as gracefully as she could (not easy with a fish tail!), leaning over the side of the sleigh drinking in the sights she had never seen before. Her hair stuck together in mucky clumps, her tail was cut and grazed with patches of missing scales and her arms and face were bruised and dirty.

"Are you ok?" I enquired gently.

She turned to face me and beamed. "Yes. Surprisingly, I am. I can't wait to go home."

I smiled back. I felt so proud that we had been able to end her and the Queen's nightmare.

The sleigh began to head towards the sea and I briefly wondered how we were going to stay in and not float away once we were underwater. I needn't have worried. Just before the seahorses dipped beneath the gentle waves, a bubble encased the sleigh. As soon as it had sealed us in, we plunged into the clear waters and the seahorses raced each other, pulling us faster and faster downwards, speeding towards the palace.

We zoomed past a multitude of colourful sea life until, at last, the palace appeared ahead. The seahorses slowed, the domed entrance hall opened to allow us in and finally, we touched down with a smooth, perfect landing. Filling the hall were mermaids of all shapes and sizes and, as the bubble of our sleigh disappeared, our ears were filled with the happy sound of clapping and cheering. We really had done it!

<u>Chapter 20</u>

Lots of things happened at once: the six mer-guards we had met earlier approached us; the seahorses were released from their reins and we all clambered out of the sleigh, painfully aware of just how many people were watching us. 'Please don't fall, please don't fall,' I repeated to myself in the privacy of my head.

Whatever magic allowed the mermaids to survive and move within the palace instantly reached the Princess. She was able to follow us out of the sleigh which, as soon as we were all out, shrank back to its original size and fell to the floor with a little clatter.

I looked properly at my friends for the first time since we had left the cave and my heart ached to see their beaten, tired bodies. They both wore scratches, bruises and cuts across their faces, arms, and hands. Violet's long hair was thick with dirt and Amelia's short hair stuck up all over the place.

They looked back at me and I saw sadness flicker across their faces, as it had mine.

"Oh Lacey, look at your face!" Violet walked briskly

to me and held me tight. I had forgotten about my bloodied nose; it caught her shoulder as I hugged her back and I jumped with the pain. Amelia joined our hug, which was slightly awkward given we were all still holding our Bonds.

The purple-eyed mer-guards approached us and, still surrounded by applauding citizens, we all walked across the marble floor to re-trace our path back through the palace to the Queen.

The grand door opened and there was Queen Beatrice. When we had first seen her, she had oozed sadness and grief but when her eyes fell upon her daughter, her beautiful face broke into a broad smile that spread from ear to ear and lit up her sparkling eyes.

Queen and Princess flew towards each other with arms outstretched. They embraced and tears of happiness poured down their faces. Speeding along behind the Queen was a turtle with a beautiful, sparkling multi-coloured shell. Its little flippers flapped as it raced to get to Lacey.

"My beautiful girl." sobbed the Queen, as the turtle bounded around Lacey like an excited dog. "My beautiful girl."

"Mum." Princess Isla sniffed into her mother's hair before reaching a hand down to rub her hand over his shell. "Hey Jerry!" She snuffled, splashing tears onto his shell as she scooped him up in her arms. "He's my Bond." Although Isla was still hugging her mother and the turtle, she just about managed to explain that Jerry was her Bond.

We stood quietly in the background until the Queen lifted her head and beamed at us. She held her daughter in one arm and beckoned us over with the other.

There was a pause as Queen Beatrice looked us over, one at a time, her smile never failing.

"My children, look at you. I know you are battered and bruised but you stand here before me as heroes. You have achieved more in this one journey than some people will in a lifetime. I am so, so proud of you and cannot thank you enough. The Succurro Spell chose well." She paused as her eyes landed on our Bonds and, for the first time, her smile wavered.

"Oh," she breathed gently. "I'm so sorry. Please wait here one moment." The Queen turned and sped down the long room leaving us suspended mid conversation.

She seemed to be having a quick and whispered conversation with one of the mer-guards. The guard exited and the Queen returned.

"Come, sit." She gestured to a set of comfy looking chairs and as we gratefully sat, we were finally able to truly relax. From an invisible door in the wall, an orangey-red crab scuttled in balancing a tray on its wide shell. It used its claws to place the tray on the table in front of us and disappeared back through the door, its legs click-clacking as it went.

From the tray, the Queen poured steaming mugs of sweet tea that warmed us throughout and a plate piled high with delicious biscuits filled each of our by now, very hungry tummies. Princess Isla curled up next to her mother with Jerry settled on her lap whilst the Queen asked us question after question about our perilous journey. We all shared our experiences with her and, by the end, she held her hand over her heart, her mouth wide.

As we neared the end of our tale, the mer-guard reappeared and behind him flew the fairy that had revived us after the poisonous bubbles. Flying with her were three other fairies and each of them had a leather bottle slung over their backs. The fairies fluttered to us and set their bottles on the table alongside the tea and biscuits.

"You did it!" Blossom squealed in excitement. "Well done. I'm so proud of you. The Queen sent for us and we came immediately. Each of you help your Bonds to drink the liquid. It will help them heal."

"Is it the same stuff we drank after the poisonous bubbles?" I asked.

The fairies nodded as they uncapped each of the bottles. Almost before our Bonds had taken their last sip, they started to stir in our laps. Eye lids fluttered and legs stretched. Piggins and Plum spread out their wings and all four creatures yawned. Within moments, our Bonds were sitting up and joining in the conversation as though they had never been hurt. Titch and Plum were crawling and flapping happily around Violet's head, who was giggling with joy. Amelia was holding Piggins tight to her, tears tracing clear tracks through her still-grimy face. I faced Pedro, unable to find the words to thank him for the huge sacrifice he had made back in the cavern. His strength and courage had saved us, and I didn't know how to express my gratitude. I rubbed a thumb over the stump of his unicorn horn and cupped his soft face in my palm.

"It'll grow back." He smiled at me. "Just takes a bit of time, that's all." I smiled back at him in relief.

Whilst we told our Bonds everything that had happened, the Queen offered the fairies tea and biscuits, which they accepted, smiling happily at the scene playing out in front of them.

With Pedro held close to my side, I turned to the fairies. "Thank you so much for coming so quickly. Thank you doesn't seem quite enough after everything you've done for us; I wish there was something more we could do."

"Lacey, you have done more than enough! If anything, we owe you! You and your friends have saved our world from being ruled over by a cruel and greedy man. You are heroes! Saving your Bonds was the very least we could do. It is our absolute pleasure," replied Blossom passionately.

"You're welcome." I replied, blushing furiously. "What will happen to Prince Thomas?" I asked, suddenly remembering the last time we'd seen him he was still lying on the floor tied up and stuck behind the table.

"Some of the guards will bring him back here where he will be held in our prison to pay for his awful crimes. I will need to arrange a conference to discuss who will take the throne once I have passed on. Obviously, it will be a someone from the land and hopefully someone far more deserving than Thomas!" The Queen replied.

I leant back wearily into the soft cushions and gazed at the underwater scene above me. As before, sea life drifted lazily through the crystal waters and I felt a huge sense of peace watching them. Before, I hadn't been able to appreciate fully the beauty because my mind had been on the daunting task ahead, but now I was able to drink in the stunning bright colours, all the different shapes and sizes of the creatures above. My body and mind were completely exhausted, and I felt like I could have stayed there forever. I let the joyous sounds of the people around me wash over me and cuddled Pedro, enjoying the comfort I got from his warmth and softness.

"Darlings, you look absolutely exhausted. I think it is time for you to return home." Queen Beatrice announced. "Before you leave though, I have gifts for you as a thank you for the great goodness you have done here."

"Stand up please." asked Princess Isla through a smile. We stood, wobbling slightly from tiredness, and faced the Queen and Princess. One by one, the Queen took something from Isla and approached us. She draped a necklace around each of our necks and then stood back.

"As a thank you, each of you now own a magic shell. Any time you want to return to Mostomsia, just tell the shell and it will open up a door for you to pass through. However, use it wisely and not often. The shell has limited magic."

We looked at each other with wide eyes and even wider grins. Our very own magic entrance to a secret world! Wow!

We were all absolutely stunned, this clearly showing on our faces.

"You're welcome." laughed the Queen, but then her face turned serious. "You have shown courage far beyond your years. You have faced dangers, challenges, and horrors that braver people than you would have turned away from. However, you loved, supported and helped each other, which gave you strength beyond imagination. And with this strength came the return of my daughter, which in turn brings safety to my kingdom and our world. How can we ever thank you for that?"

We stared at her, the reality of what we had achieved finally starting to sink in. I just nodded at her, tears prickling my tired eyes.

The Queen and Princess came to each of us and embraced us warmly, murmuring thank you in our ears. We hugged them back and then it was time to go home.

"I hope to see you soon!" called Isla, as the mer-guards led us away. "Thank you again!"

We were approaching the door when I suddenly remembered something. "Wait!" I shouted before turning and sprinting back to the Princess. "I found this when we were looking for you. Here." I grinned at her as I handed over the bracelet I had found on the black-sand beach.

Princess Isla beamed at me, took it from my hand with cool fingers and thanked me again before I jogged back to my friends, waving good-bye over my shoulder.

<u>Chapter 21</u>

We travelled back through the palace one final time, to the entrance hall where the shell waited to return us back to the shores.

My eyes felt heavy as the shell rocked gently in the water, but my mind was too full of our adventure to switch off and before long, we were back at the beach.

Pedro led the way back up the path with Piggins and Plum flying happily through the trees and around our heads. Titch swayed contentedly on Violet's shoulder listening to our conversation, which rolled from topic to topic, not staying long on anything.

"How are you going to explain your nose to your Mum?" Violet asked me.

I clapped a hand to my mouth; I hadn't thought of that. "I have no idea! We've all got some explaining to do, look at us!" I cringed at the thought of explaining how we'd managed to scratch and bruise ourselves so badly when we were supposedly tucked up, poorly, in bed.

We spent the rest of the journey trying to figure out

what stories we could be tell our families and it wasn't long before we could hear the rushing waterfall.

Pedro walked through first, closely followed by Piggins and Plum, who flew through spinning as they went, clearly enjoying the feel of the water on their wings.

Amelia walked through and Violet followed with no hesitation this time. I took one last glance around the clearing, soaking in as much as I could. I smiled and walked through the water, once more enjoying the feel of it on my skin and hair.

There was one last surprise when I walked out the other side: Amelia and Violet both looked as though nothing had happened at all! Their bruises, cuts,

bumps and grazes had completely vanished, their hair looked fresh out of the hairdressers and their clothes looked like new. From the looks on their faces, the same magical transformation had taken place for me too.

"Oh yeh, I forgot to mention that didn't I?" giggled Pedro, seeing our looks of utter shock.

"It would have been good to know! Instead of panicking about our parents!" Amelia laughed back.

We passed through the cave and out into the clearing we had first arrived in; it looked just as vibrant as before and I could have sworn the pink colour of the flowers was even stronger.

There ahead was the enormous tree that we had come through and, to our utter amazement, there stood the wooden door, waiting for us.

Before we opened the door, we stood in front of our Bonds. They had each sacrificed so much for us and now it came to say goodbye, I was filled with sadness.

I knelt so I was eye-to-eye with Pedro and stared at him silently. Beside me, Amelia had knelt to Piggins' height and Plum was hovering in front of Violet and Titch.

I pulled Pedro into a tight hug, trying to show him how grateful I was for everything he had done. I felt warm tears flow down my face into Pedro's fur and I felt like a hand was squeezing my chest. I didn't want to leave him behind. I hadn't met him that long ago but I felt like I'd known him forever after the experiences we had shared. He was my Bond after all. We all stayed, holding our Bonds for a long time but eventually we pulled apart. As we did so, a huge, beautiful rainbow spiralled upwards away from each of us, raining tiny sparkles down upon us.

I put my hand on the black handle of the door and pushed and there, ahead, was my bedroom. My computer, my fairy lights, the bean bags, and popcorn just as we had left it. It felt as though we had been gone forever and not been gone at all.

We turned to wave one last time to our Bonds before stepping through and closing the door behind us.

?? **Chapter 22** **??**

I plopped heavily onto a beanbag and turned to ask Amelia a question. But she wasn't there. Neither was Violet. I felt panic flash through my chest and leapt up at once. I rushed out of my bedroom calling

out for my mum, who appeared in her bedroom doorway.

"Lacey! What on earth is the matter?!" she asked me sleepily. "It's two o'clock in the morning! Why are you dressed?!"

I faltered, unsure of what to say. "Umm... err..." I stuttered. "Umm. Bad dream?" I mumbled. "Sorry, I'll just... umm... back to bed." I turned round and sped back to my room before she could ask me anything else. I was so confused. I had no idea what day it was, let alone what time it was!

I reasoned there was nothing I could do now so I put on my pyjamas, climbed into bed and fell fast asleep, hand grasping my new, special necklace.

I woke up the next morning feeling more confused than I'd ever felt in my life. What day was it? I looked at my clock to see that it was eleven o'clock and, by the light streaming through my curtain, it was daytime. I wondered why that hadn't occurred to me when I'd gone rushing down the hallway last night.

I stretched my limbs and was considering snuggling back under the covers for some more sleep before I suddenly realised that Violet and Amelia had vanished.

I leapt out of bed and thundered down the stairs.

"Can I use the phone please?" I almost shouted at Mum through my panic.

"Morning to you too! Glad you seem to be feeling better. You've been asleep since Friday evening! You must have needed it."

"Yeh, loads better." I responded absently, more focused on finding out where my friends were than having a conversation with Mum. "Can I use the phone?" I repeated.

Without answering, she handed me the phone and I began dialling Amelia's number. At that moment, the doorbell ring and I heard Mum saying: "Morning girls, do come in. She's just woken up."

"Morning Mrs Bell." I nearly fell over with relief. There were Amelia and Violet at the front door, their voices floating in on a warm breeze.

I flung the phone back on the side and rushed to my friends before practically dragging them upstairs back to my room.

"Did it really happen?" Violet whispered excitedly. "Did it really?"

"It did." Amelia whispered back as I nodded frantically.

"It really did." I added.

We spent the day talking about what we had done, reliving each moment. As the sun set, they went home, leaving me alone in my bedroom once more.

~ ~ ~

Right at the beginning, I told you I had two huge secrets. One of them was that my bestest best friend is a unicorn and the other is that I have a magical shell that will open a door to an alternate reality where I am friends with mermaids.

I suppose now, there is a third secret: in that world, my friends and I defeated an evil prince and a terrifying beast to successfully rescue a mermaid Princess.

Would you tell your Mum?

Printed in Great Britain
by Amazon